GREED

THE CHARITY DEACON INVESTIGATIONS BOOK 2

P.A. WILSON

FREE EBOOK

Claim your copy of Buying Into Death when you use the QR code to sign up for my newsletter and follow Charity as she solves her fastest case yet!

ONE

It had been three months since Jake went to Morocco to make a movie. Three months of emails and phone calls, and a growing feeling that I was losing him.

My work as a private investigator hadn't been fascinating since I'd finished with the people traffickers. I'd had a couple of wandering spouse cases. One of them wasn't even wandering. He'd forgotten to tell his wife he was going fishing. I was getting pretty tired of boring cases.

I'd taken the leap into adulthood and decided to stop dabbling in investigating and actually put some effort into my business. Charity Deacon Investigations now had a website. I had a business coach and a five-year plan. But right now, I had a lack of business. When Jake called to say he was given a week off filming and would I like to spend some time with him in Paris, I jumped at the chance.

When I told Lu, she said, "Let's get out of this freaky spring chill and add on a week in the South of France. You'll be better for the break and I'll get a vacation."

We were leaving in six hours.

I had my passport, some euros, and an empty suitcase. And

a pile of clothes on my bed that was too big to fit in the case. I still had time to get a bigger suitcase, but something told me that I would just find more things to bring with me.

I made a pot of coffee to help me think. When I had my mug in hand, I decided that I should make a pile of the essentials; clothes, toiletries and put other stuff to the side.

When I was done, I was staring at the pile of clothes, which might now fit into my suitcase, when the doorbell chimed. Thankful for the interruption, I headed downstairs.

Standing on the finger dock was Delores Markham, neighborhood gossip and rule keeper. I readied myself for some kind of lecture. A quick glance over Delores' shoulder showed me Lu making her way toward us. Unlike me, Lu was looking chic in black and cream. Tall and slim, and perfectly groomed, she always looked elegant. It wasn't just because she was rich, or Asian, there was something cool inside her.

I was tall, but built a little more solidly, and I lived in jeans and tee-shirts. Today, I didn't have to check in the mirror to know I was looking harried and messy.

I looked back at my neighbor and hoped my taste never went to heather and beige outfits. "Come in, Delores," I said, keeping my voice cheerful.

I left the door open so Lu could just walk in. Since gang members broke into my little floating home and trashed it, I had the door set up to lock when it closed. It meant I had to keep a spare key in my car, but I slept better knowing I couldn't accidentally leave the door unlocked.

"Thank you, Charity," Delores said, pulling her cardigan around her as if she was cold. "I understand you are going to France today."

Lu walked in and went straight to the kitchen. "Can I pour you a coffee, Delores?" she asked.

"No, thank you, Lu." Delores smiled as she spoke which kind of put me off kilter.

She had been so nice to me when I got beaten up and came home to find my house a disaster zone. I knew there was a nice Delores in there, an interesting one even. It just seemed she preferred to show the world the judgmental Delores. Or maybe Lu was right, and the judgment was all in my mind.

"Yes, we're off to France. I'm just packing. Is there something I can do for you?" I tried to convey a feeling of urgency without seeming to push her out the door.

"Yes. I would like to ask you a small favor. I have a friend in *Pina sur Midi*. It's a small town on the Mediterranean, near Cassis. Will you be going in that direction?" Delores' voice caught on the last question. This was more than a small favor. I looked a little closer and noticed shadows under her eyes. Delores was worried enough to lose sleep.

I pulled one of the chairs out and asked her to sit. "We'll be close enough to go. What's the favor?" I waited. The tension she wore like a veil didn't shift.

Lu put a box of Kleenex on the table and joined us. At least I wouldn't have to deal with an emotional Delores alone. I hoped she didn't need the Kleenex. I didn't like tears at the best of times, but tears from her would be like the sphinx sobbing.

The words came out in a rush. "Well, my friend, her name is Audrey Wylie, hasn't been in contact for a few days."

"Have you talked to the police?" I figured she was going to ask me to find this Audrey, but I wasn't going to barge into a French police investigation.

"Yes," Delores said. "Of course, I did. The Gendarmes were not very helpful. However, they said they would look into it. A gentleman by the name of Matthieu Durant is in charge of the case."

I could at least try to talk to him, but before I promised, I wanted all the information. "Is it possible that your friend just went away for a few days?"

"She would have told me. Charity, I know there is some-thing wrong. Audrey and I have been friends since we were activists in the sixties. She never lost that drive to fix problems. I know I have grown too old to join protests. But Audrey could never pass up an opportunity to right a wrong. She is quite inspiring."

I ignored Lu's raised eyebrow. I'd tell her what I knew about Delores' history with the Equal Rights Movement later.

"What exactly makes you think something is wrong?" I prompted. Delores was like a lot of my regular clients. The emotions they felt fought with their thinking. Like they could only be logical if they were calm. I was used to prodding until I got what I thought was everything.

"She said she was sure someone was running guns in her town. She told me smuggling was a problem in all the coastal towns, but lately there had been incidents that she thought were more than the normal cargo of marijuana or alcohol. She said that someone might be watching her." Delores dug into her purse and handed me a sheaf of printouts. "Here are all her emails and the information I gave to Mr. Durant. Please, Char-ity, it would mean a lot if you could make sure the police are taking this seriously."

Who could say no to a scared old lady? It wouldn't hurt to check with the local cops and maybe have a poke around. In fact, doing that would let me write off some of the cost of the trip.

"I can pay you," Delores said, misunderstanding my hesitation.

"No, you don't need to do that. I was just thinking of the best way for us to check. Do you have her address and phone number in here?" I held out the papers.

"Yes, it's on the top page. Thank you, Charity, it means a lot to me." She turned her attention to my home and the worry seemed to slip from her. "I feel like I should be doing something in return. Can I keep an eye on your home while you are gone? And Jake's?"

Despite feeling that I was giving her permission to snoop through my things, I said, "Yes. That would be great. The house sitter I contacted still hasn't gotten back to me, and I don't have time to track her down."

I pulled out my spare keys, Jake's was on there, along with my front door and car. "You don't need to do anything but pick up the mail."

When Delores left, Lu looked at my packing attempt and laughed. "It'll all fit, don't worry." She started rolling the clothes and stuffing them in layers into the case. She looked at the pile of other things I'd set aside. "Why are you bringing your laptop?"

"We might need it for emails or something." *And playing solitaire when I get bored.*

"Leave it here. If we need to be in touch, we'll find an internet cafe."

I started to argue but realized I'd be lugging the laptop with me on the plane, train, and rental car. I decided to go for an unencumbered ride.

TWO

When we arrived yesterday, Lu and I had taken the TGV to Avignon and stayed there overnight. Now, after a couple of hours driving on the motorway, we were finishing lunch in a bistro on the outskirts of *Pina sur Midi*. I was already in love with France. Even the suburbs looked like they had been here for a thousand years. It was hot compared to Vancouver, and the sun was welcome. Plane trees were everywhere, lining country roads and standing twisted in the parks we drove by.

Lu put down her coffee cup and called for the bill before saying, "If we keep eating like this, I'll need to start exercising."

Lunch had been mussels and fries, it sounded so much better as *moules and frites*, and a shared dessert to go with the light and refreshing *rosé*. I dug in my purse for the GPS. "Not me. I am going to eat and drink as much as I want. I'll diet when we get back."

We paid the bill. I checked the route to town and lost a little of my holiday buzz. "This looks a bit crazy." I showed Lu the route, which was a tangle of twisting roads and roundabouts. "Let's go to Audrey's first. That way we only have to go into town and find a room, and we don't have to drive out until we leave. Remember the guidebook said to head for the center of town and there would be plenty of hotels."

We followed the GPS to a small house. It looked like a gate-house from a period movie, all pale stone walls, blue Mansard roof, and a heavy wooden door. An ancient wisteria draped itself across a lattice, the lilac cones of blossom swaying in the breeze. There was no doorbell, so I lifted the heavy iron ring and dropped it. The door swung open.

I took a step forward, and Lu grabbed my arm. "Are you sure you should just go in?"

"We could call the cops," I said. "I don't know how long it will take them to get here, though. Delores didn't seem all that impressed with them, and you know how she respects authority."

We tiptoed into the small vestibule, and I stopped so abruptly that Lu almost bowled me over. The inside of the house was a disaster zone. I knew it wasn't a robbery. It reminded me so much of what Jag Chen had done to my home that it must be a warning.

"Charity?" Lu stood with her hand over her mouth. "Should I call the police now?"

"Let's have a look first. If they didn't notice this mess, it's either recent, or they really haven't come by and looked for Audrey. I want to make sure she's not hurt somewhere in that mess before we get stuck answering questions."

The living room was in front of us, so we started there. The couch was ripped, the curtains torn from the rod. Papers were everywhere, some ripped, and some just smashed into a ball and tossed away.

"Be careful you don't trip on this," I said to Lu. I really wanted her to wait in the car, but if she was with me, I wouldn't be worried that something had happened to her. "We'll go through the house once and then call the cops. Or better still, go to them."

The study was buried under a blizzard of paper. Here they'd torn pages from books, and the library shelves had been tossed. The chair and desk were turned over but seemed unbroken.

The powder room was a mess of towels lying in a pool of soap and water. In the dining room, there were a few broken plates on the floor. The only other room downstairs was the kitchen. The damage was confined to a few papers that had drifted from the living room when we opened the door. You have to love the respect the French have for food.

There was no one under the mess. I left Lu downstairs and ran quickly to the second floor, another mess, but no Audrey. I tried to give that a positive interpretation. No body, so Audrey could be okay.

"Do you know if 911 will get the police here?" I called to Lu as I came back down. "This is definitely not just a weekend away kind of thing."

When she didn't answer, I hurried to the living room to see a man in uniform waiting. Lu was standing in a cleared space near the window.

"Madame, I am pleased that you would feel it necessary to inform the gendarmerie that you have entered a place that is clearly a crime scene."

I couldn't believe he was going to pretend we were at fault. "I'm surprised you didn't already know it was a crime scene. This woman has been missing for a week, and you only now come to see what has happened?"

MY ILL-JUDGED comments got us a ride to the station and what was already an hour sitting waiting to be interviewed. It didn't look any different from a Vancouver police station. The walls were painted a color that might have been cream at some point, but now was faded to a gray-yellow that just depressed me.

I must have looked pissed off, because Lu said, "We'll figure it out. Don't worry; it's not your fault we're here. I would kill for a coffee, though."

I thought it was a bit foolish to say you'd kill for anything in a police station, but she was right. And I was getting hungry. Mussels are tasty, but they don't exactly stick to your ribs.

I nudged Lu. "What do you think would happen if we left to get a snack then came back?"

I followed her gaze around the waiting room. Any gendarmes in sight were busy talking to each other, or to a couple of hardened men who were clearly criminals. The other people sitting and waiting were ignoring us. I could almost hear their disdainful 'tourist'.

"We could make a run for it," I said. "Just think, an espresso and pastry. Or maybe a chocolate? Or some ice cream."

"Stop." She smacked my arm, none too gently and laughed. "I don't want to spend the night in jail. And we still need to find a hotel. Try to be helpful when they ask us questions. And let's make it as quick as possible."

"I promise. Hey, maybe we can get a hotel recommendation." I looked at the reception desk. There was a lull in the people hanging out there. There were limits to my patience. I needed to do something. "Be back in a second."

The woman behind the desk was blond and wore little makeup. I wasn't exactly a fashion diva, but she would look ten years younger with a touch of lip gloss and mascara.

"*Oui, Madame.*" she said when I had her attention.

"Do you speak English?" A phrase I'd found very helpful over the last two days.

"Of course," she said in that French way that makes me feel stupid, both for thinking she didn't, and for not speaking French myself. "How can I help you?"

I looked at the nametag she wore, Dominique Girard. "We are waiting to speak to Officer Matthieu Durand. Do you know when he might be available?'

"*Inspecteur* Durand is in a meeting. It may be some time." Most of the time, the French corrected you without attitude; this time the correction came with a thick layer of 'idiot'.

"Do you think it will be okay for us to go and arrange a hotel and then come back?" I didn't mention the fact we'd need a cab to Audrey's where the car was, and we'd stop for a snack, and maybe it would take a couple of hours before we got back.

"It would be better if you waited. I am sure it will not take much longer." She turned back to her computer.

"Then we'll be back in a few minutes." I wasn't asking permission to go get coffee.

She nodded and returned to the computer screen.

"Let's find that coffee," I said when I got back to Lu. "It won't take long."

She gathered up her purse and jacket, and we headed for the door. "I saw a place just down the block."

"*Mesdames* Deacon and Cho?" A male voice called just before we made it outside.

Lu turned and started back. I swore under my breath and joined her.

I assumed this was Matthieu Durand. He was about my height, and blond, with those icy blue eyes that sometimes looked gray. He carried a weariness in his face that was somehow charming. His clothes were rumpled, in a very French chic way.

He looked at us and smiled. It made him hot—not as hot as Jake—but definitely in the top ten of men I knew.

I turned to say something to Lu. My mouth snapped shut. She was blushing, and I saw a shine in her eyes that had been missing since her husband died.

If Matthieu Durand could make my best friend look that alive, then I'd cut him whatever slack he needed.

We followed him to an office. "Please, have a seat. May I get you a coffee?" His voice was a little rough as though he'd been a long-time smoker. But he didn't look like a smoker – unlike what seemed like the majority of people in France.

"That would be pleasant," Lu said before I could answer. "We were just thinking of going for one when you called our names."

Oh, man. Lu had that high tone to her voice, the 'I'm speaking to a guy' voice.

Matthieu called and asked Dominique to bring us coffee. When she brought the tiny espresso cups with a chocolate on the side, I thought she was developing a twitch. She looked at Matthieu like he was a cold beer on a hot day, and at Lu and me as though we were something she'd scraped off her shoes.

As soon as we were alone again, Inspector Durand took out a notebook and started asking questions.

"Have you been in France for long?"

"We arrived yesterday morning." Okay so maybe it wasn't the hardnosed interrogation I expected, but I wasn't planning to give him any information he didn't ask for.

"Ah, you must be experiencing the jet lag." He made a note while he spoke. Then he looked up and focused those great eyes on Lu. "Have you enjoyed your visit?"

Lu smiled at him. "Up to the point where we tried to visit a neighbor's friend, yes. Ms. Wylie seems to have run into some problems."

Good girl. Never let the hormones get in the way of reaching your goals.

"I suppose the break-in happened after you checked on her," she continued.

I watched some expression cross his face. Maybe something was lost in translation, but I could have sworn it was annoyance, and not directed at me for a change.

"Your neighbor?" He pulled a file up on the computer. It didn't come up fast enough apparently because he sighed in annoyance, definitely annoyance. "Ah, yes, Madame Markham. She contacted this department to say she had not heard from Madame Wylie and asked that we visit her home to ensure she was not in danger."

"Yes," I said, joining Durand in his annoyance. "I am interested in what you found. Mrs. Markham had not heard back from your department, despite her repeated emails." I pulled out the sheaf of papers from my purse.

He took them and put them on the edge of his desk. "There have been other priorities. We were able only today to visit Madame Wylie's home."

I bit my tongue. It wouldn't help for me to say they wouldn't have even come today if some nosy neighbor hadn't ratted us out.

"Then it is fortunate that we were also able to visit today," Lu said. "Perhaps you would have had other priorities if we hadn't seen the mess. I assure you we were about to call the police ourselves. I wonder if any of her neighbors were as vigilant on the day the break-in happened."

I totally had to learn that. If I had said the same thing, it would have made things worse. Lu managed to bring a smile to Inspector Durand's face. Maybe the batting of her eyes made the difference.

"Yes, it is fortunate, as you say," he said.

I decided to ride the wave of good feeling. "Inspector

Durand, can you tell us anything that we can pass on to Mrs. Markham. She is very worried."

"Please, call me Matthieu. *Inspecteur* is not a rank in the gendarmerie." He answered my question but looked at Lu the entire time.

I wondered if Dominique thought that telling us a bogus rank would make us look stupid. I guess being on a first name basis was a good sign, though. "Fine, Matthieu, and the information?"

Matthieu finally turned to me. He straightened up and seemed to pull a professional coat on. "We have nothing more than you found. I am going to assume you did not do the damage and so, you are free to go. If you would like to leave your information, I will provide you with an update when we do."

So, suddenly we were all business. "We will stay in town until we have information. Can you recommend a hotel?"

He was about to answer – I wasn't sure if it would be a huffy 'I am not a tourist bureau' or a recommendation – when the door to the office opened behind us. I turned to see a much older man with an immaculate uniform on. It contrasted with the rumpled look Matthieu sported.

"Lieutenant Durand, when you are finished, you are needed in the Colonel's office." I'm not sure why he spoke English, but it seemed like he wanted us to know he was important.

"I will be some time, still, Sargent. *S'il vous plait, fermez la porte.*" I could have sworn that we had been dismissed a minute ago. Perhaps we were and he had other work he needed to do.

Matthieu turned back to Lu. "Now, *Mesdames*, I can recommend a hotel. But, first, I believe your car remains at Madame Wylie's home. Perhaps I can drive you there?"

"Thank you," Lu said. "I'm sure you are far too busy to drive us around." She stood as she spoke and smoothed her capris.

"But perhaps we can revisit the house and you can explain to me what you have discovered – if anything." He shut down the computer and gestured for us to leave. "And you can tell me why it is your neighbor was so sure that her friend was in danger."

He led us to the garage where we climbed into what was obviously his personal vehicle, a beaten-up Renault. I flicked a glance at Lu and then jumped into the back seat.

As we were leaving, a uniformed gendarme strode forward, hand raised to stop the car, but Matthieu stepped on the gas a little and gave a cheerful wave as though he didn't realize they wanted him to stop.

THREE

We arrived at *chez* Wylie a few minutes later and Matthieu removed the seal from the door. Inside, it was worse than when we left it. In addition to the mess already there, fingerprint power made black blotches on every surface, and now the kitchen was in disarray. I don't know why the cops would have messed up something that wasn't broken into, but the contents of the cupboards were now on the counter.

"Please, after you." Matthieu held the door open for us. "If you can try to remember what you first saw, perhaps you will notice something out of the ordinary."

"But we didn't know her. How would we know what was out of the ordinary?" I looked around anyway as I spoke.

Matthieu cocked his head at me. "Ah, but you are a private investigator, are you not?"

I turned away from my inspection of the living room at his words. "How do you know that?"

He smiled and said, "I googled you. The picture on your website is very professional."

Well, I guess the money I paid for the website was worth it.

Lu returned from the small study behind the staircase.

"Will someone arrange for this to be cleaned up? I hate to think of her coming home to this. You know what that's like, Charity."

I did, and when it happened to me, I hired cleaners. Maybe there was a version of Molly Maid here.

"It is not normal for the gendarme in charge of the investigation to arrange for cleaning the scene." Matthieu gave a shrug that encompassed shoulders, hands, and facial expression. Now I knew what the Gallic shrug was.

Lu looked at me, and I knew we'd be talking about how we made sure the house was clean. "And what does the victim usually do?" I asked Matthieu.

He looked around the room. "I believe they have friends, or a service, come to assist."

"Are they usually victims of kidnapping?" I snapped. I regretted my tone as soon as the words were out, but his disinterest was getting on my nerves. How could Lu like someone this unconcerned about how Audrey would feel coming back to this mess?

He held up a placating hand. "Let us discuss this cleaning later. We do not yet know if Madame Wylie is kidnapped. I promise I will assist in whatever way I can."

Before I could say anything more, Lu touched my arm.

She asked, "Can we come back at some point? We're hungry and tired and need to get into a hotel."

Matthieu nodded. "I will arrange for you to have access tomorrow morning. I think it would be prudent to do this as soon as you can."

I kept my mouth shut. Lu obviously had a reason for putting this off, and I wasn't going to mess it up.

"Thank you." She took my elbow and we returned to our car.

"Can you give us the address of the hotel?" I pulled out the GPS.

Matthieu leaned in to speak, "There is no need for that." He flicked a finger at the GPS. "It is simple to find. Drive along this road until you reach the roundabout, take the first exit, and continue until you see the hotel. Please tell them I sent you." He handed me his card. "When you are settled, come back to the station, and I will provide you with the instructions on how to let us know when you are ready to return here."

Lu leaned across me and flashed her best smile. "I'm sure we will be there within the hour. But if not, how late are you available?"

"I will be at the station until eight this evening. If you are later than that, please call the mobile number on the card."

I waited for him to drive away before I started our car and my questions. "What the hell are you up to? We could have gone through the house in ten minutes and then been done with the police."

Lu shook her head. "Wait until we get a room, and I'll show you. Besides, I'm not sure I want to be done with this particular policeman."

I groaned and put the car into gear. "Okay. We get a room, and we check with him. Then I want a dinner in a bistro with wine and dessert and all the trimmings. No matter how cute he is, we are not hanging around the station so you can make goo goo eyes at him."

She laughed. "Yeah, yeah. I'm hungry too. While we're out, we might want to get a couple of phones. I checked with my provider and it's a fortune to make calls with our Canadian plan. We're better off doing one of those preloaded each."

We found the hotel and Matthieu's name got us a discount, but no extension on the days. We only had two nights. If the Audrey problem wasn't resolved within that time, we were going to have to find a new place to sleep.

We dragged our suitcases up the narrow stairs and dropped

them on the floor in front of the twin beds. I wondered if mine was long enough for me to sleep in. It looked like a kid's bed. I turned to Lu who had her case open. "Okay, show me what you have. It had better be good."

Lu reached into her pocket and retrieved a small black-leather bound notebook. "I found this in the study."

I flipped it open. The pages were filled with notes written in violet ink. "How did the police miss this? Actually, how did whoever tossed the place miss it? And why didn't you hand this over to Matthieu?"

She flopped down on the bed. "The police and the criminal missed it because it was tucked into a dark corner of her desk. Well really, it was behind what looked like the side of the desk. It was a false side."

"And what made you look there?" I was flipping through the pages. Mostly numbers, a code or schedule, maybe.

"Mark had an old French desk, and it had a hidden compartment exactly like Audrey's. I figured it would be worth the effort to look." Lu was unpacking as she spoke.

I looked at my case and unzipped it. At least my clothes didn't need ironing. I looked around. There was no bureau, only a small closet. "I'll leave my stuff in the suitcase. You take the closet. Tell me why you didn't give the book to Matthieu."

She blushed. "Well, I don't think the police are giving this the attention it deserves. You know Delores wouldn't have asked for help if she wasn't really worried."

I laughed. "And you wanted an excuse to see him again."

She wiggled her eyebrows. "Yes, he's cute. And I'm on holi-day, so maybe a little romance won't be such a bad thing."

"You don't need to defend yourself. I think it's about time you had someone in your life." It made me happy that she was willing to start taking a chance on a relationship, no matter how fleeting. "I was beginning to think you would never look at another man."

"I've looked," Lu said. Then she sighed and started straightening her sweater before folding it. "I know you think I gave up on love after Mark died. But I didn't. It's just hard to..." She paused and I thought I saw a shine to her eyes. "I loved Mark like he was the only man in the world. When he died, something disappeared from my life. It's just hard to get involved when you think maybe they'll leave and take another piece of you."

I wished I hadn't started on this subject. "You don't have to do anything. I'm sorry, I didn't mean to make light of it."

"I know. But maybe it is time." She hung a jacket in the closet and then sat on her bed. "Is there anything interesting in the book?"

I tossed my pajamas on my pillow before picking up the book and handing it to her. "There are names and dates and other information. It's going to take some concentration to figure it out, if I even can. Let's go make our visit to Matthieu and then get food. I'll look at it tonight before I fall asleep from jet lag."

FOUR

The local cell phone company was called Orange, which seemed weird to me, but it was something to do with Holland. It was still open, so we managed to convey our needs to the clerk and within half an hour we each had a red flip phone with a couple of hours talk time. I wasn't sure we'd be apart enough to need them, but it was nice to know that we could call each other if necessary.

"Let me do the talking," I said to Lu as we headed toward the station. "You are more than a little smitten."

She grinned at me and nodded. "You go ahead. I'll just enjoy the view."

I glanced at her and was happy to see the shadow of grief was gone.

We walked the few blocks to the police station, checking out the four bistros on the way. "So, a holiday romance, should we have tried to get two rooms?" I looked over the first posted menu.

"I'm not ready to jump that far into the pool," Lu said. "Have you noticed how much better everything sounds in

French? *Steak Frites* is so much more tasty sounding than steak and fries."

"Yes, and in French it sounds as though it might be nutritious as well." I moved on to the next restaurant. "So, you aren't ready to jump into bed with him, but you're happy to look. It's an improvement. Let me know if you want me to disappear. I'm happy to help you enjoy your vacation."

"*Omelette frites*," Lu said. "Does everything come with fries here?"

"No. Look, there's lots of other stuff on the menu. Don't dodge the question. If we are going to be hanging around here to find Audrey, then you'll be seeing more of the lovely Matthieu. It would be nice to know whether I should give you some privacy."

"I don't think you'll have to worry about that," she said. "All these places look great. How about we just eat at this one today, it has nice blue awnings. We can check out the others tomorrow. Let's go see Matthieu." She walked away.

I turned to follow her. "Okay. But we're getting in and out. He'll tell us how we access the house for a real look through. We'll arrange to meet him tomorrow, so you'll get to ogle him. And then, dinner and wine... and dessert and wine. And then sleep. I need to catch up on this time zone. Oh, I guess I should try to decipher the book."

"Okay," Lu agreed as we walked through the door to the station. "I'll try not to embarrass you."

We were both giggling by the time Matthieu came to the lobby. "Ah, please come back to my office."

He led us to the same room we'd been in that afternoon. When we sat, I expected him to tell us how to get the key. But he didn't speak, so we waited.

After what seemed like five minutes, he leaned back and said, "I have arranged for you to have access to Madame Wylie's home tomorrow morning at eleven. Is that acceptable?" He smiled, but it was strained.

"Eleven should be fine," I said, silently wishing for Lu to start distracting him. I don't know what we'd done to make him suspicious, but he definitely had something he was holding back. "How do we get in?"

"Someone will be waiting for you. They will let you in. You will give them everything and anything you find. Agreed?"

I had a sinking feeling that what he was holding back was an accusation about evidence taken from the crime scene. But I wasn't going to do anything to confirm his suspicions. At least not until I had a chance to read the book and make my own notes. I guess there was no leeway for time zones. I might only get tonight with the book. "That's fine."

"Is your hotel acceptable?" Now he turned his attention to Lu and all of his suspicious behavior slipped away. If he only knew.

"It's lovely." I reached for my purse, ready to leave.

"It's such a pity we can only stay two nights," Lu said. "I hope we can find out what happened to Audrey before we have to leave."

"You are not able to stay for more than two days?" I saw a flit of disappointment cross his face.

I took pity on him. "No. We need to be in Paris within the week, but the problem is the hotel is fully booked. We'll need to find another place to stay if we are needed here."

"Ah, well, you will never know what is available in the future. But you are probably tired since this is your first day. Perhaps I will have another recommendation tomorrow."

I nodded and turned to tell Lu we were going to leave when the door to the office opened again. "Lieutenant Durand, *pourquoi et vous ici?*" The man who barged in was about six feet tall, thin as a wraith. He smoothed the temples of his graying hair and smiled. His expression was probably meant to look pleased and surprised. It failed.

I don't know how different office gossip was in France, but I was pretty sure that everyone knew we were here. Even if they didn't know who we were.

Matthieu stood. "Colonel Fitzroi, allow me to introduce Madame Deacon and Madame Cho. They are the ladies who have inquired about our missing person."

"*Pardon.* I am sorry to interrupt, ladies. Lieutenant Durand is needed in my office."

I hoped they didn't let him question suspects. Either he didn't care to, or he wasn't able to, disguise the contempt in his voice. If he was doing it on purpose, he was good. I couldn't pin down just who he was contemptuous of, Matthieu, us, missing women, or people in general.

"We were just leaving," I said, trying to be gracious. I turned to Matthieu to say, "Thank you, Lieutenant."

Lu had already pasted a smile on her face, and I gave her a little pull to make her stand up. "Will we see you tomorrow? When we report anything we find?" she asked.

Matthieu ignored his superior officer to escort us to the door. "I hope to be available. Please, enjoy your dinner tonight."

The Colonel stepped aside, giving us plenty of room, as though we were contagious. When we were halfway down the corridor, I looked back and saw Matthieu talking to his boss. By the frown on his face, and the clench of his fists, he wasn't happy.

WE SETTLED into chairs outside of the restaurant. It was a bit chilly now that we were in the shade, but I really wanted to eat outside. It was on my list of things to do in France. The sidewalk in front of us was wide and we had a great view of the street.

Across from us was a line of small shops and a bakery. No 7/11, no Starbucks; we were definitely in a different world.

I closed my eyes for a second to try to make myself shift from Vancouver to France. Go from comparing things to just enjoying them. The background chatter was a different cadence. The traffic sounded different, more treble than bass, and there were scooters everywhere. And smokers, the tables outside the restaurant were filled with smokers. It kind of spoiled the experience.

"Charity?" Lu's voice broke through my thoughts. If I'm honest, it woke me up. Jet lag is a bitch.

What hadn't been on my list was find a missing senior citizen. I wanted to put a check mark against that as soon as we could. The problem was we were definitely in a different world. Unless we lucked out, I was going to have to familiarize myself with the town before I could seriously hope to conduct an investigation.

When the wine came, Lu and I tried to organize our time around the case.

I put aside the idea of two days — well, one now — and said, "I guess we really have eight days to solve this if we need to. I just hope we'll have some tourist time. There are cathedrals and *chateaux* waiting for us."

Lu laughed. "Fingers crossed we'll be done before we lose the hotel room. Do you think we should check out the other hotels just in case? Or, maybe, we could stay at Audrey's. If we could do that, we could clean it up for her."

I almost said, forget it, but then had second thoughts. "If we could get permission. It might help us figure this out if we were in her house. We could talk to the neighbors, get a good handle on what she was up to just before she disappeared."

Lu poured more wine into our glasses. "We can ask tomorrow, when we give Matthieu what we found."

"What you found. Anyway, I think if you give Matthieu a big smile, he'd let you do anything you want."

Lu leaned forward; her voice quiet. "Do you think I'm making a fool of myself?"

If she was worried about people overhearing, it was more serious than she wanted to admit. Shyness usually meant Lu had something to risk.

I paused while the waiter placed our appetizer on the table. A platter of meat and cheese with a sliced baguette each.

"I think it's time you gave yourself a chance to do that. Despite the fact you have been in mourning this long, you aren't the type to stay a widow for the rest of your life. If you feel attracted to him, I'd say give it a go and don't worry about what people think. Sometimes making a fool of yourself is the best thing to do."

She picked some cheese off the plate and layered it with a slice of sausage on a piece of baguette. "What about you and Jake? Are you ready to make a fool of yourself?"

"We're definitely attracted to each other." I picked up some cheese and nibbled it to keep my mouth occupied.

"You know what I mean. Are you feeling committed?"

"I don't want to lose him. I've missed him. But that's a long way from commitment. I don't want to be the little wife standing in the shadows." My appetite faded with the thought.

Lu almost choked on her bread and meat. "I don't think Jake is expecting you to be a shadow. At least, I can't imagine him wanting a shadow."

I signaled the waiter to bring us another bottle of wine. "I'll think about it. Maybe watching you flirting with the French Lieutenant will help."

FIVE

We had breakfast in the hotel, and despite the amount of wine we consumed last night, neither of us had hangovers. The coffee was excellent, and I ate a few too many little croissants – they were filled with dark chocolate, how could I resist?

We checked in with the receptionist before heading out. She was charmingly apologetic, but there were no cancellations. She said she would call other hotels to see if there was another room.

I turned to Lu. "I need to burn off a few calories. How long do you think it will take us to walk to Audrey's house?"

"We've got an hour and a half. I can't see it taking any longer than that. Even if we stop and shop." Lu picked up one of the tourist maps. "It's in the suburbs, so it might not be on here. Do you know how to get to the house?"

I had spent some of the time in the car trying to memorize landmarks and directions. If we were going to be here for our whole vacation, I wanted to get to know the place. "Yes, if we walk, it's only a couple of turns. There are a lot of one-way streets so it looks way more complicated on the GPS."

Lu ran upstairs to change into more walking appropriate

shoes, and I grabbed the GPS from the car. A little searching around the menus yielded a walking option. I dropped it in my purse. If we got lost, I'd resort to getting directions.

"No matter what happens this morning, I want to head down to the harbor tonight," Lu said waving a brochure at me when I got back. "There are restaurants and shops open late, and it's all tiny wandering streets."

I hoped we would find something in the house that gave Matthieu a clue. Otherwise, the guilt at not investigating would spoil the exploring. Then I remembered I was going to have to know the town. "Actually, maybe we could do both. I mean, normally, I'd be trying to figure out what the missing person did with their time."

Lu steered me toward the door. "Good idea. I'm sure some people around town knew Audrey. We can spend our evening asking about her in restaurants and stores. And there's a market the day after tomorrow. I am not leaving France without going to at least one market."

We formed a plan on the way to Audrey's. I'd been right about the route, so the GPS stayed in my purse. We passed an *InterMarché* – the French equivalent of Safeway – and picked up rubber gloves, all-purpose cleaner, and a package of garbage bags, so we could start cleaning up as we looked through the rooms.

As we left the town center behind, the streets changed from rows of stores to tightly packed houses, then to larger houses with walled front gardens. A few trees showed over the top of the walls, some with pink, and some with yellow, flowers cascading from the branches.

The only other stop was to have coffee and shared pastry at a tiny bar. I know, I know, walking off the calories was not supposed to include adding calories.

A cop car was parked outside the house and the front door

was open. Lu hurried through the gate, I'm pretty sure she was expecting Matthieu to be there. "Wait," I said, as I grabbed her elbow. "We don't know the cop is inside. It could be anyone. Let me look first."

"Why? Do you have a gun?" she asked, but still let me get in front of her.

"Not a gun, but I have a much heavier purse than you do. Stay out here, if I don't call you in, run and find help." I handed her the grocery bag and sidled forward.

I was nervous, but I figured the odds were high that the cop was inside. The thing is, I don't like playing the odds when entering a crime scene, so I came to the door from the side. Trying to make myself a small target.

I looked through the door into the vestibule. There was no one there, so I stepped inside and pressed against the wall. I still didn't see anyone, but the noise of someone shifting furniture came from the study.

I held my purse by the handles, ready to swing it at the head of any attacker. The GPS making a nice hard lump at the bottom.

The noise stopped with a final thump, probably the couch landing back on its feet. I tiptoed across the living room toward the study, trying to keep the staircase between me and the person in there.

I was almost at the door. I could hear someone grunting as though they were lifting something heavy.

Then my purse announced, "At the end of the road turn around."

I didn't know whether to run into the study or out of the house. As I made up my mind, I saw a man emerge from the study. I swung the purse back in one sweep, and then almost wrenched my shoulder when I registered the uniform. Fortunately, I stopped short of assaulting a cop, or gendarme, or whatever they were called.

"Madame Deacon?" He didn't seem to notice he'd almost been brained. He was young, maybe mid-twenties, dark hair, high cheekbones, and brown eyes. He looked a bit uncomfortable with the authority of the uniform.

"Yes," I said then turned to call Lu into the room.

My purse said, "Turn right when possible." There was something in the tone that made me think she was annoyed. But that was crazy.

I dug around until I found the damn GPS and pressed the off button. "Sorry, I didn't realize it was so easy to turn on."

"I am Alain Marchan. I have been attempting to bring some order to this mess." He looked at the bags in Lu's hand. "Ah I see you have the same idea. It will be easier for you to look for information as the Lieutenant expects, if we, how do you say, tidy up."

I looked at his uniform and wondered if he would be willing to get dirty. That fingerprint powder was going to be a bitch to remove, and it was likely to transfer. "Thanks. It will be great to have someone do the heavy lifting."

"Perhaps, as you look through the room, I can clear the way." He pointed to the study.

"I think it will be faster if we split up," I said. We didn't need supervision. If we found something, I might not want to hand it over right away.

"Are you in a hurry?" he asked. "I think we will work together better than apart."

That nagging feeling that the cops knew we had evidence came back. It was as if he'd been told not to let us out of his sight.

Lu slipped past me into the study as I answered, "Not really a hurry, but wouldn't it be better to know as soon as we can if there are any clues here?"

His cheeks flushed, and I knew I'd won. He pointed to the study and said, "Perhaps if you start in there, I can prepare the rooms ahead of you."

I was happy to compromise as long as we weren't under his scrutiny. "Let Lu start in the study. I'll have a quick look in the kitchen. When we were here yesterday, it was not in that state."

The kitchen didn't reveal any hidden compartments, or secrets tucked into the various jars and canisters. I left Alain putting things back and went into the study.

"Let's start with the desk. Maybe there are more secret places in there," Lu whispered before kneeling and starting to prod and knock on the wood.

"I'll go through the books." Most of them were on the floor. I started with the ones left on the shelves, flipping through the pages, and returning them to their place. Then I picked up scattered ones and restocked as I flipped through each one. No secret safes hidden inside. No hollow sounds when I knocked on the back and sides of the built-ins as I filled the shelves.

We'd finished our search just before Alain came in. "The kitchen is back in order. Did you find anything here?"

Lu gave me a sideways glance, and I just nodded. This time, she needed to hand over whatever she'd found. We were going to be in enough trouble when they found out about the notebook.

"These seem like legal papers." She handed him a folder that was filled with cream colored, heavy bond papers. "They are in French, though."

Alain took the file and flipped through the contents. "Yes, it is a will and a *procuration*, what you would call a power of attorney. Perhaps they will disclose a reason for someone to do this to an old woman."

We moved on to the living room then the bathroom. There was nothing downstairs that we could find. I followed Lu upstairs glancing back to see Alain spraying cleaner on the light switches to remove the fingerprint powder. "He'll make some woman a great husband if he cleans up that willingly."

"It's kind of weird that he's going to this much effort for someone he doesn't know, don't you think?" Lu pushed open the door to the upstairs bathroom.

"And what are we doing? The only thing we know about Audrey Wylie is that she was a friend of Delores back in the day." I peeked over her shoulder, a nice bathroom and it didn't look disturbed.

"Yes, but we know Delores." She moved on to the first of three other rooms. This one was a bedroom; it had been tossed like the other rooms downstairs. The second door opened to reveal a large linen closet and the third a small guest bedroom. Both were a mess.

"Why don't you start in the main bedroom?" I said. "It's getting late and we still have to meet Matthieu. I'll do the bathroom and guest bedroom."

Lu found some jewelry in the bedroom, but other than that, we didn't find even a dust bunny.

Alain came up and between us we made both beds and shifted furniture back into place.

"The lieutenant is expecting us; can I drive you back?" Alain pointed to the cruiser. We climbed in the back and returned to the station.

While we waited for Matthieu to join us, his boss wandered into the lobby. If we were supposed to think it was by accident, he must have thought we were particularly stupid.

"The Canadian ladies." He was clearly trying on a jovial personality today. "Do you remember me? I am Colonel Fitzroi. It is a pleasure to see you again. But not so nice for you, I think. Surely you must be anxious to continue your travels."

I preferred the snooty attitude he wore yesterday. This happy face was a bit creepy. "Yes, we are hoping to visit some of your country's famous buildings, but it's important that I put my friend's mind at rest."

He seemed to think that over for a second. Then a smile crossed his lips. "But you must not let Lieutenant Durand impose on your time. I assure you; we have this little mystery in hand. Madame Wylie will be found."

"He is not imposing." Lu stood. "We're happy to help."

Matthieu moved from behind Fitzroi to stand beside Lu. "Ah, thank you Colonel for entertaining the ladies while they were waiting. I fear our lobby is not the most inviting place."

"Durand." The Colonel nodded. "I was just suggesting that they would prefer to visit more of France, and we should not detain them."

Matthieu waved a hand dismissing the suggestion. "Oh, but they have been most useful. Did I mention that Madame Deacon is a private investigator?"

The Colonel gave me an appraising glance. "No. But I must remind you that you are not licensed to investigate here."

I just nodded in response. I didn't want to get into what was obviously a battle of wills between Matthieu and his boss.

The Colonel said his goodbyes and we followed Matthieu into his office.

"I apologize," he said. "Some of my colleagues are territorial. Is that the correct phrase?"

"If you mean they don't like people digging into what they think is their business, then yes." I saw the folder of papers sitting on his desk. "You've had a chance to look at what we found."

He opened the folder and placed the documents on his

desk. "Yes, Madame Wylie's will, and various other papers. I do not think they will help us find her, but the power of attorney will solve one problem, I think."

Lu sat forward a little in her seat and said, "It's unfortunate we didn't find anything that will point you to solving the case. I was hoping to be more help."

Matthieu kept his eyes on the papers, as though they would protect him from her wiles. "I am sure if there was something there, you would have found it," he said. "Gendarme Marchan says you were most thorough in your search. I understand the house is in a better condition now that you have finished."

"We tried to be thorough, and Alain was so helpful. Thank you for sending him to meet us," Lu said.

This was the weirdest flirting I'd ever witnessed. I think I need to give her some tips. Tip one; don't compliment another – younger – man when you flirt.

I tried to take control of the conversation. "You said the documents can solve one problem."

"Ah yes, the power of attorney. We will assume Madame Wylie is alive so that it is still a valid document, I think. It seems that your neighbor is given the authority to make decisions for Madame Wylie. I can contact her if you would like and have her give permission for you to stay in the house. This will solve the problem of your hotel."

I looked at Lu. It would be nice to have the house as a base, but since someone had already tossed it, there might be a bit of danger.

"Do you think it will be safe?" she asked before I could voice the same concern.

"I cannot be certain, but whoever broke in has done a very thorough search. The jewels left behind were valuable, and so we must assume it was not a robbery." He shrugged. "We will patrol the area more frequently, but I think you will be safe."

"Why don't you make the call?" I suggested. "We can talk about it tonight and let you know."

"Very well, and what is your plan for this evening? I hope you are going to find time to enjoy our town."

Lu leaned forward again. She had that part of flirting down pat. "Yes. We are going to look around the harbor and eat there tonight. Do you have any recommendations?"

His face lit up in a smile again. "You must try to eat at the *Bistro Mistral*. My cousin Pierre owns it. Please let him know I sent you."

SIX

We were back in the room, changing for walking around and dinner. I pulled the GPS out of my purse because we wouldn't need it tonight. The harbor was down the same street as our hotel. Even we couldn't get lost.

Lu plunked herself down on the bed and said, "Whew, I don't know how you do that."

"What?" I said as I dug into my suitcase for a jacket. "We didn't do anything but talk to the cops."

Lu grimaced and said, "Keeping secrets from the police."

I stopped my search for a suitable jacket and looked at her. "What secrets exactly and why did you need to keep them? And why didn't you tell me?"

She pulled sheets of paper out of her purse. "Okay. Answer one, these are the secret. I found them in the linen closet. There was a loose floorboard. I needed to keep them because I think the cops are trying to sweep something out of sight on this. And, answer three, when would I have been able to tell you?"

I took the papers. They were actually printouts of pictures. "Fine, I guess you're right." There were only three of them. The first was a picture of crates of guns, the other two of streets. "It looks like she was trying to tie the guns to a place. One of these doors is probably the location of the gun stash," I said.

"Do you think that we should hand them over to Matthieu? Along with the book?" She sounded much more relaxed now that the secret was out.

"I don't know." I stared at the pictures of streets trying to memorize them. If we could find the location, it might help to move the investigation along. "I think you're right about the cops. There's something going on there — or rather nothing is going on that should be. It's like Matthieu is the only one who thinks there's something to investigate."

Lu took a turquoise linen jacket from the closet. She'd unpacked and spilled the contents of her jewelry bag on the bureau even though we would be moving in a day. "I know I was the one who took them, but now I'm feeling guilty that we have two clues that might help find Audrey."

"And you don't like holding out on Matthieu, right."

Lu shrugged, but I could tell it was an act. She was too cool. "True, but I don't know how to do both. Find Audrey and come clean to Matthieu."

"It's not the best way to start a relationship," I said, still looking at the pictures.

"Maybe this isn't a relationship. I guess I can only deal with reality right now. Audrey is missing and the police don't seem to care. This thing with Matthieu might not be anything."

I didn't know whether to hope she was right about Matthieu or not. I decided to leave the subject for now.

"Look, we can fix this. I didn't have time to read through the notebook last night. I guess one more day won't hurt." I stuffed the printouts into my purse. "I'll bring the notebook and the pictures. Maybe these streets are down at the harbor. We'll look when we get down there. And then at dinner, we can try to figure out what's in the notebook. Whether or not we figure out what it means, we'll give both to Matthieu in the morning. You can come up with a reason we didn't hand them over right away."

"Why me? You are the one who lies for a living." The panic in her voice made me laugh.

"Oh. I could take offense at that. But you're right, I do spend a lot of time convincing people to tell me things. I just don't like to think of it as lying."

She laughed. "Okay, creative use of the truth, how does that sound?"

I grabbed my black fleece jacket. "Okay, we'll both think of something. Come on, let's get going."

The harbor was like a postcard. Boats filled every slip and the streets radiated out from the water. That is, they radiated out until the first turn then the cross streets twisted off at angles, and I could see how easily someone could get lost. We relied on the fact that downhill was going to get us somewhere near the harbor if we lost track of our landmarks.

We didn't see any streets that looked like the pictures, but we only made it around about a quarter of them before it got a little too dark for my comfort.

At about eight, I'd had enough. The streets were deserted, my stomach was wondering if my throat had been cut, and we hadn't made any progress. It was disconcerting to be in such a different landscape. These streets were lined with stone walls broken by painted shutters and doors, not a tree in sight.

We'd walked a block past the last closed storefront when I grabbed Lu's arm. "Look, I think we're done. How about dinner?"

Lu nodded, and we turned around to head downhill.

I was proud to find out that I remembered each turn, when we came on the harbor front only a couple of blocks away from where I thought we should be. The street that ran along the harbor was called *Quai des Baux* and it was a row of one restaurant after another. The scent of onions, garlic, and butter tickled my nose.

"What was that bistro Matthieu told us to try?" I asked.

"*Bistro Mistral,*" Lu's answered quickly enough that I wondered if she remembered everything that Matthieu had said. "Is that it?" She pointed to a dark blue awning that covered tables full of happy diners.

"It looks full. Maybe we won't get a seat." I glanced at the other restaurants, they all looked perfect, and a few of them were only half full.

"We won't know until we try." Lu marched toward the crowded patio.

When we mentioned Matthieu, there was a flurry of activity, which resulted in a small table at the edge of the sidewalk being made available. It couldn't have been more perfect if we'd come early enough to have our choice of tables.

As soon as we sat, a man appeared with a bottle of *rosé*. "Ladies, Matthieu called to let me know you were coming. I am his cousin, Pierre. Please, accept this. It is a local wine. I hope you enjoy it."

Lu thanked him and introduced us. "Do you have any recommendations for our dinner?"

Pierre smiled at this. "If you will permit, our chef will prepare something special."

When we agreed, he left to inform the chef. I said a little prayer that we wouldn't face sweetbreads or something equally scary. I put it out of my mind and told myself to just enjoy. "I could get used to this," I said, taking a sip of the *rosé*.

Across the street was a small marina with brightly painted fishing boats tied up in a row. And just past that, a view of the Mediterranean, and a perfect sunset. Music and laughter and a lap of water against stone completed the ideal vacation evening.

While we waited for the first course, I pulled out the note-book. "I did look at this last night, but I was totally wiped, so I couldn't make any sense out of it."

Our appetizer of mussels with *Pernod* sauce arrived. And the waiter topped off our wine.

When he left, I continued, "If we assume these are dates, I think she was recording deliveries. If I'm right, then they are probably deliveries of guns." I stopped talking to sample the food. It was orgasmic. The mussels were fresh and carried the tang of the sea. The *Pernod* sauce rounded out the flavor with the taste of licorice. "This is worth the jet lag."

Lu was using an empty shell to dig the orange meat out of her share of the mussels. She looked elegant. I was using a fork and felt like a peasant, but I was used to that. She stopped picking and said, "So, if we can find the street, we can guess when the guns will come through?"

"Yes, but I think we're looking for Audrey, not for guns. Unless you think she was kidnapped by the gunrunners?" As I said it, I realized that's exactly what must have happened. "Find the missing woman, find the gun runners?"

Lu nodded and started to speak but closed her mouth as the waiter reached to take our plates. He came back an instant later to replace the *rosé* with a bottle of white.

When he finally left, she said, "So do we walk the streets again tonight? Are you feeling up for it?"

Before I could answer our waiter placed our entrees on the table. Roasted fish with potatoes. The aroma made my mouth water. I took a few bites before I realized how quiet it was. I looked up to see Lu smiling around a mouthful of fish. Suddenly I didn't feel like such a peasant.

I put down my fork and sipped the wine before saying, "I'm fine, but I think we'd be better off looking during the day. That's when the pictures were taken. I'd hate to miss it just because it looked different at night."

"You know, the market is a day away —"

Pierre was at our table. "Ladies, please I am sorry to interrupt you. I hope the food is to your liking."

I smiled and answered him, "I don't think I've ever had anything as delicious."

He beamed. "I will tell the chef. I hope you will have room for a desert."

We assured him we would find room.

When he was far enough away, Lu continued, "The market is tomorrow. Look at these pictures. There are stalls along the street. I think they were taken during a market day."

I nodded. "Yes, and if they set up the tables the same way every time, we could try to find the sequence of vendors."

"Let me see the notebook," Lu said. I handed it to her and finished my meal as she flipped through the pages. "If you are right, then this means there's a shipment due in a couple of days. That is if the pattern stays consistent."

We flipped through the notebook while we waited for dessert, but nothing else came to mind that would help us find Audrey.

Suddenly, Lu sat straighter in her chair and slipped the notebook back into her purse. I turned to see Matthieu coming toward us. "Good evening, ladies. I hope you have enjoyed the evening."

He pulled a chair from a nearby table and joined us, motioning for the waiter to bring him coffee.

I sat back and watched how Lu would play it.

Matthieu's eyes flicked to where Lu's purse sat on the floor. Then he turned his gaze back to her. "Did you find a hotel for the rest of the week?"

That feeling he knew about the book and pictures almost

had me blurting out a confession. I managed to clamp down on it. He wasn't stupid, but for some reason he was giving us a lot of leeway. I couldn't believe that reason was Lu's flirtation.

"No. There are none available according to the receptionist at our hotel." Lu pushed her purse under the table with her shoe. "Were you able to contact Mrs. Markham? If we can't find a hotel through the week, then we'll need to stay quite a way out of the town."

His coffee arrived and Matthieu put two packets of sugar in before answering, "Yes, I had a very interesting conversation with her. She has agreed to you staying at her friend's house but would like you to telephone her this evening if possible."

I nodded. Delores deserved an update anyway.

"Do you have the key?" Lu asked with a smile.

Matthieu frowned and gave his head a little shake. "I think it is unwise to put you in the house right away. We don't know who might have access. We have arranged for the lock to be changed, so I know you will be safe. It is a pity, because if Madame Wylie is simply on vacation, she will not be able to enter her house. So, we must find a way to leave her instructions on entering, but I'm sure you will have some ideas."

He stared at his empty coffee cup. I couldn't tell if he was waiting for us to give him an idea, or if he was trying to think how to ask what we were hiding. Or, maybe, I was being paranoid. He could just be thinking of a way to ask Lu out on a date. Maybe the problem was me. I was cramping his style.

"You're right, we'll think of something," I said. "Maybe one of her neighbors will hold a spare key."

"We will ask," Matthieu said. "I am sure they would be happier to know from the police what is happening rather than some stranger."

The feeling I was in the way wasn't fading. I didn't see any indication that Lu noticed, so it was time to test my theory. I shifted my seat back and stood. "I'll be back in a few minutes," I said as I headed for the bathroom.

There was no real place for me to stand and spy on them, but they weren't paying any attention to me. So, I stood a little out of the way and watched.

Matthieu and Lu sat talking with their heads close. Lu was fiddling with her hair, and Matthieu kept touching her hand. So, at least, part of his behavior was about Lu.

"They seem very happy, yes?" Pierre said. He stood at my side, and we both watched them for a few minutes.

"I should go back," I said.

Pierre touched my arm and said, "Your friend, she will be kind to Matthieu? When she leaves?"

I looked at him. I was wondering about Lu being heart-broken and hadn't even given a thought to Matthieu. "She is not going to break his heart on purpose. Is he easily broken?"

Pierre laughed. "Ah, that is not my worry. He is not so easy to fall in love. He has not looked this happy in a long time. Please, do not let my question spoil your holiday."

When I returned to the table, the two of them were laughing and Matthieu seemed more relaxed. I decided to stop waiting for him to demand we hand over the evidence.

"Matthieu has ordered us some cognac," Lu said, glancing at my chair and raising an eyebrow. I got the message. She wanted me to stay.

"Lovely." I parked my butt in the chair and decided that it was time to try to get information from Matthieu. "How is the investigation going?"

"Ah, it goes slowly. It seems that there is no clue for us to follow, so we are still trying to find out from neighbors and friends what might have happened."

I read that as he wasn't getting support. It was pretty clear he was the only one who thought this was a priority. "Are there criminals in the area? Perhaps she stumbled on a drug deal, or a murder." I tried to be careful about spilling how much information we had. We needed the notebook and pictures one more day. Then I'd find a way to 'discover' them.

Matthieu shrugged and waved his arm to indicate the entire harbor. "It is a port city. There are always criminals to be found. You must know that, Charity. You've had experience with this, yes?"

He'd already admitted to doing some research on me, so I guess he knew all about the people traffickers I'd dealt with a few months ago. "Yes. I guess easy access gives criminals the opportunity to bring anything into the country, people, drugs, fake designer purses."

He nodded and paused while the waiter left our balloon glasses of cognac on the table. "And guns and many other undesirable things. It is disappointing that the house did not reveal anything for us to use."

I flicked a glance at Lu and saw she had a guilty look on her face. If he turned away from me right now, he would know we had something.

"Do you think Audrey got involved in the something illegal?" I asked more to keep his attention on me than because I had any doubt. "Do you have informants in the gangs who can tell you anything?"

"If we have to ask, we will. It seems we do not wish to expose our people for little reason." His voice had tightened. I figured there was more resistance to the investigation than we saw in the office. "But it is early in the investigation, and it is possible something will reveal itself."

Lu had control of her expression, so I just nodded and hoped they'd get back to flirting. No luck. Matthieu gave me a look that almost had me confessing again. I wondered if he had the same success with real criminals.

Matthieu continued, "It is often the case that someone has dismissed a fact or observation that turns out to be important."

"Matthieu." Lu touched his arm again. "When will we be able to have the key? It would be helpful to get into her house and have another look around."

"I expect the locksmith to be finished by ten o'clock. Perhaps you can come to the station by eleven? That will give us time to prepare the neighbors for your presence." He sipped his drink. "Enough of this business talk, I would like to take you both for dinner tomorrow. Perhaps you will have found something by then? I will come to the house by six, yes?"

Our desserts arrived and we ended the evening talking about the town. And Matthieu promised us a local perspective the next day.

SEVEN

The next morning, we finished packing and checked out of the hotel. Last night I'd gone through the notebook again, but still couldn't get anything concrete out of it. Eventually, we decided it was time to give Matthieu the book and the pictures. If we had to, we could pretend we found them when we moved into Audrey's house. Neither of us wanted to lie. But I liked the idea of being free of the guilt more than the idea of being charged for withholding evidence. And who knows, Matthieu might find something we couldn't.

"So, we'll drop off the cases and then go for supplies," I said, loading our stuff in in the back of the car. "I want to get out to the harbor before it's too late."

She handed me the last bag. "If we have to meet Matthieu at the house by six, we need to be fast. Maybe we can suggest he meets us in town. That way we can look around more."

I got into the driver's seat and pointed the car toward the station. "Good idea. If we give him the evidence away from the house, we won't have to lie about exactly where we found it."

I glanced at her and saw the stress around her eyes. "What

bedroom do you want?" I hoped a change of subject would do some good.

"I don't care."

"Okay. Well you take the master then. You need the closet space. And, you never know…"

That got a laugh out of her. "Okay. Let's get the key, and then stop and get some groceries. It would be nice to have some meals at home now we have one."

The drive from the hotel to the station was pretty short, only a few blocks, but we had to go the long way around to find parking. I found a spot a block away from the station. The book and printouts were packed in with my clothes. I didn't want to chance it falling out of a purse before we were ready to hand it over.

"Lieutenant Durand is in a meeting," Dominique informed us. I got the distinct feeling that she would prefer he stayed in the meeting until we left.

I pointed to the plastic chairs lined up against the wall. "He's expecting us, so we'll just wait over here."

She nodded, and I swear she sniffed as soon as we turned away.

"You might want to be careful," I said to Lu. "I think you have competition for the attention of the French Lieutenant."

"I got that feeling too. But really, it's up to him who he flirts with and we'll be gone soon, so she can have him to herself again." Despite her flip words, Lu sounded disappointed.

The only thing I could do was give her permission to dump me to spend more time with him. "There's no reason you can't stay here while I'm in Paris. I get the feeling you won't make much romantic progress until we solve this case. So, why don't you think about staying for the rest of the time? Just meet me at the airport for the trip home."

"Let's hope we figure it out fast then," she said. "Seriously, thanks. I'll think about staying. I would like to spend a little more time with Matthieu. Time that doesn't include a case to solve."

I laughed. "Careful, talk about solving cases might lead to being addicted to crime busting." Lu glanced behind me. I followed her gaze and saw Matthieu approaching. "I'm sure he has time off. You know, I could pretend to get sick tonight and let you have the evening together."

She laughed and stood. "Good morning, Lieutenant."

"Please, do not be so formal." He smiled at her and pointed at the door to his office. "Let us talk in here."

Dominique glared at us as soon as Matthieu turned away. I decided then and there to make sure Matthieu and Lu had a real date before we left. That woman behind the desk was way too possessive to allow her to have Matthieu all to herself.

We settled in the office and Matthieu opened the file on his desk. "I have been meeting with my superior this morning and we have a conclusion to this case."

"You found her?" I felt a surge of hope. Sure, we had nowhere to stay, but it meant we could leave town. Well, maybe not right away. After all, Lu and Matthieu needed to go on that date.

"No. We have not been successful in contacting Madame Wylie. The Colonel has arranged for messages to be left on her mobile phone, and we have given instructions to her lawyer to make contact if possible." He sat back and started squaring the papers on his desk.

"So, we are still needed," Lu said. "If she hasn't been located, how do you have a conclusion?"

"There is no reason that you cannot stay in her home for the rest of your visit, but I am instructed to tell you that the official investigation is closed. From the information we gained through discussion with her neighbors, Madame Wylie frequently leaves her home for short visits around the country. We conclude that this is what has happened. It is unfortunate that her house was vandalized while she was away, but it seems, from what her lawyer says, she has insurance to cover the costs."

He spoke quickly and seemed happy to have finished his official speech. Lu raised an eyebrow, and I knew she wasn't buying this anymore than I was. It was time to leave, but I wasn't letting him off the hook. Partly because I didn't think he wanted to be let off, and partly because I was not going to face Delores with that half-baked theory.

"I think we'll stay a few more days, perhaps she will come home in the meantime. Will you still show us the town tonight?" I smiled invitingly.

Lu leaned forward and added, "I would love that, please say yes."

"I would not think of disappointing you. Shall we meet at six as agreed?"

"We are going to wander around this afternoon, why don't we just meet at the harbor?" Lu batted her eyes at him. I swear she was going overboard and braced myself for his laughter.

Matthieu didn't seem to mind. He just smiled and agreed to meet us outside his cousin's restaurant. He gave Lu the keys to Audrey's house, and we left the station, chased by the glare from the reception desk.

When we arrived, we dragged our suitcases upstairs. Lu took the main bedroom, and I got the guest one. "Get unpacked and we'll go get some breakfast food." I didn't want to turn this into a domestic situation. We were on vacation, and I wanted restaurant food, but it would be nice to start the day drinking coffee in my pajamas.

We agreed to meet back downstairs in fifteen minutes. I finished in ten, so I started a grocery list: bread, wine, coffee, and chocolate – all the essentials.

When Lu came down, she had the pictures and notebook in her hand. "What are we going to do with these?"

I sighed. It had been in the back of my mind all morning. When Matthieu told us the case was closed, I almost had Lu slap them on the table to say here's a reason to reopen it. But the way he said it, made me think there was more to the story. Like it would stay closed even if we dropped a bloody knife on his desk and a video of someone stabbing Audrey.

I took the pictures and fanned them out. "It feels wrong to keep them. We could copy these and give Matthieu the originals, but he'll just put them in a closed case file."

"And it's not really possible to copy the notebook," Lu said as she dropped it on the counter. "If there was a printer here, we could do it, but I don't think we can stand in the French version of Kinkos for an hour. And it would cost a fortune."

"We haven't really gone through it in detail." I flipped through the book again. Audrey had written on both sides of the sheets so there were almost a hundred pages of tightly written notes. "If we don't hand over the evidence to Matthieu, we could do that tonight. Get into the details I mean."

She sighed. "I hate to keep things from him. But you're right. The gendarmes don't seem to be interested in investigating this. If we hand these over to them, it won't restart the investigation. Every time I look at Delores in the future, I'll feel guilty about not doing enough."

I could already feel the cringe that would come over me if I had to tell Delores we couldn't find Audrey. "So, we're in for as long as it takes?" I looked at Lu.

"What about Jake? He's expecting a week of romantic Paris with you." She picked up the grocery list and said, "Let's get this. We can talk while we shop."

"I am really hoping it will only take us a few days. But if I'm in for the duration, he can come here." I hoped he would be willing to change plans without me having to grovel. "It's a pretty town, and we can be romantic anywhere."

I put the book and photos in the cutlery drawer and followed Lu to the car.

I thought about how we could move the investigation along as Lu drove to the *InterMarché*. When we had our cart, I started sharing ideas. "We need to find the locations in the pictures. It's definitely down by the harbor, based on what we saw yesterday."

Lu stopped at a display of artisan sausages. "It also makes sense for them to keep the guns near the harbor, if they are bringing them in by boat." She took a few sausages off the display and put them in the cart. "If we get these, we'll have something to give guests. We could get cheese and some fruit, too."

"Guests? I'm not sure that we'll have time for cocktail parties." I winked at her. "Unless you mean one guest in particular, a certain lieutenant."

She blushed. "And, maybe, the neighbors. We need to get to know them. They might fill in a gap or two in our knowledge."

She was right. Teasing Lu was fun, but we had a woman to find in a strange town where we didn't speak the language.

Lu started filling the cart and talking. "This is making me hungry. What if we head into the harbor after unpacking and grab a bite before we spend the rest of the afternoon finding our way around the streets?"

I started loading wine bottles into the cart. "I will feel better if we are actually doing some investigation. I hate to complain since we have a place to stay, but a hotel is chore free."

Lu put two loaves of bread in, and said, "Yes, but with the house we get to try all this great food."

I surveyed the contents of our cart. My small shopping list had grown to what looked like six bags of groceries. "We should make a sandwich at home instead of eating out. Otherwise, I don't think we are going to be able to get through this stuff in a few days. If we find her soon, Audrey'll get a windfall of food along with her rescue."

Lu added a bag of fruit to the basket. "Okay, but maybe we should try knocking on some doors too."

I started to argue for going down to the harbor, but this time my brain kept me from telling her and turned my reaction into a question. "Why? I thought you agreed that we should go searching the streets for the doors in the picture."

She pointed me to the closest checkout. "We might have more luck if we get some information. Don't you think we spent enough time wandering around yesterday?"

"I'm starting to wonder if you're angling for a job as an investigator. I was thinking we could do it tomorrow before heading to the market, but you're right, we have more time right now. We don't meet Matthieu for four hours. It would be nice to have something to tell him when we do."

"Don't feel you have to keep him updated on our progress for my sake," she said. "Until he tells us what the hell is going on, I don't feel like he deserves any information."

"You are such a hard-ass." I laughed. "You might want to remember he would make a good source of information for us."

EIGHT

After lunch, I stuck a couple of bottles of water in the car and then we proceeded to knock on doors. The houses on either side were empty, or whoever was home wouldn't answer the door.

"Let's cross the street before we go to the house on the other side," I said. "The closer they are the more likely they know something helpful."

Lu shrugged and followed. "Should we split up?"

"No. I think it would help for both of us to be there if we do get someone to answer the door. It's good to just observe sometimes."

The house directly across from Audrey's was surrounded by a walled garden filled with mature shrubs. From the street, the house was barely visible. When we entered through the black iron gate, we could see the same stone building, but it looked like it had really been there since the 1600s. There was moss on the shaded parts of the house, and a grapevine that hugged it like a long-lost lover.

I banged the knocker and we waited. The shade was cool, a nice change from the street. After a moment, I heard someone shout, "*Oui oui, je viens.* I'm almost there. Don't go away."

Lu looked at me. "English, thank goodness."

"Really English by the sound of it," I said as the door swung open.

"That I am," a man said. He was in a wheelchair with a large cast on his right leg. "You must be the ladies staying in Audrey's house. Come in. I can make a cuppa if you have time. Name's Reginald Black, you just call me Reg." He wheeled away. Lu and I followed, closing the door behind us.

"Just park yourselves in there. I'll be back in a tick and we can have a natter."

In there turned out to be the living room. It was cozy, brown leather, and blond wood furniture surrounded by bookshelves. A stereo in the far corner played New Orleans jazz.

Lu sat on the couch. I wandered the shelves trying to figure out what Reg was like by the books he kept. It didn't help — unless he was afflicted with multiple personality disorder, Victorian children's stories sat side by side with Isaac Asimov and Jane Austen.

"Right. Now if one of you can take this, we can pour the tea." Reg had a tray balanced on the arms of his wheelchair; his elbows bent wide to turn the wheels.

Two minutes later, we'd introduced ourselves, the tea was poured, and we all had cookies. Lu sat back, and I took that as my cue to start asking questions.

"We're trying to help the police with the investigation into Audrey's disappearance," I said. "We were wondering if anyone saw anything suspicious."

Reg sipped his tea and a wrinkled his brow. I suspected he was enjoying the attention. "Why do you think the police need help, dearie?"

Tricky question. I wasn't going to trash the cops to him. You never know who's best friends with the local police. "It's more a favor for a friend. I live next door to a woman Audrey has known for ages. She asked us to help. I'm a private investigator, so she thought I would know how to find Ms. Wylie."

He perked up with that. "A lady PI, how intriguing. I love a mystery. Well, the police have everything I know about what happened before she disappeared. But don't bother asking, I didn't see anything."

"Is there someone we can talk to? Someone the police might not think to ask?" I felt a bit rude to push, but I didn't want to spend any more time visiting with Reg unless he had some leads. "It's been a while since she went missing. I'm worried."

Reg dipped a cookie in his tea and munched it. I hoped he was thinking, but I'd bet money he was stalling. Lu and I returned our cups to the tray, and I started to rise.

"No need to go in a huff," Reg said. "If I could get about, I'd be looking for Audrey myself. She is a very sympathetic lady. You should talk to Guy. He runs a tapenade stall at the market, and they were friends. Liked a bit of tapenade on her toast, Audrey did."

I settled back on the couch. "Thank you, Reg. I think that will be helpful. Do you have any ideas what happened to her?"

We listened to Reg's theories for a half hour and then excused ourselves to knock on a few other doors. No other neighbors were home, so we went to the harbor.

IT TOOK us a couple of hours of searching, but at the end of it, we stood on a steep street lined with storefronts. The sun was reflecting off the light stone sidewalk. Down the hill, a cafe doing a bit of late afternoon business, and a few cars driving by were the only evidence that people lived here. We stood in front of a faded blue door trying to look like we weren't casing the joint.

The door looked like it hadn't been opened for years. It

faced south and the sun had sucked the life out of the paint, but it matched the picture I held down by my hip. Lu glanced around and asked, "Do you think we might be able to hear what's going on behind there?"

"Maybe if you stop looking over your shoulder every few seconds, people wouldn't notice if we hung around long enough to listen." I was tired, and lunch was long burned off, so I didn't have a lot of niceness left in me. "I didn't notice any way to get in behind. If we have to check it out from here, we're stuck doing it under the eye of any neighbors."

I looked around the street again. There were apartments above the stores across the street, so we could very well be under scrutiny. "Let's have coffee at that place down the hill and watch for a while."

"Okay." Lu started walking and looked more suspicious by trying to be casual.

I needed to get her to relax and actually be natural. I gently pulled her to the window of a jeweler and pointed to something hanging on a display rack. The shop owner was busy with someone inside, but she looked up and smiled at us. I smiled back and said, "Relax, Lu. I'm sorry. I know it's hard, but if you don't relax, people will call the cops."

I felt her breathe out and the she lost the rigidity. "Look at that bracelet. Do you think it would make a good present for Annie?"

Ah, the power of shopping. Annie was Lu's housekeeper and she loved bangles. "It would be perfect. Why don't you go in and check it out? I'll stay here and see if anything goes on next door."

"It might be better if you went and got us seats in the cafe. It will look odd if you are still window shopping when I'm in there."

Now she was thinking. "Okay, don't be long."

She turned and entered the tiny shop. I took one more look at the door, it was weather beaten and faded, the original color was that French blue. A tarnished brass knocker and door handle were the only fixtures. No street number, no business sign, and the only window was boarded up. It could be abandoned or could be a luxury apartment. It seemed that here, people spent the money on the inside of the house, leaving the outside to look, at best a little drab, at worst abandoned.

I wandered casually to the cafe, sat at a table for two just outside the door and waited for the waiter to pay attention. The aroma of freshly drawn espresso shots perked me up even before I ordered my own.

Lu was leaving the jewelry store as the waiter took my order two espressos and two slices of the cake I saw being served to the couple at the table on the other side of the door.

We chatted about the jewelry Lu'd bought until our coffee and cake were gone. The other couple was locked into each other's private universe and I'm pretty sure they had no idea we were there.

"I guess nothing happened while I was inside?" Lu asked, much more relaxed now that she'd shopped.

"Nope, I get the feeling that door hasn't opened since the war. Maybe not since World War I."

She gave me a sly smile and said, "Well, that's because it's not the entrance."

"What?"

"I was chatting with the jeweler. I like the way people are so nice in stores here. Anyway, I said we were thinking of moving to France and were looking for a property."

Man, she learned fast, going from frozen to investigative in two seconds flat. I crossed my fingers that she'd been careful. "So, how did you find out about the entrance?"

"It just came up. We were talking about how it's not that

easy to know where the houses are and where the businesses are. The jeweler told me that it's because buildings change with the times. She said, 'this warehouse next door was a hotel when my mother was a little girl. Now it's all boarded up and only trucks go in and out.' So, I said, 'how do they do that? It's such a small door'."

Lu took a sip of the water we'd been served with the coffee. "The entrance is not the door next to her. It's the brown one at the end. Apparently, the warehouse takes up the rest of the block."

"Good work, Sherlock. I'm not sure how we can use the information, but it's better than having to figure out how to get through that door. It's probably blocked inside anyway."

"Yes, and I guess it means we aren't likely to hear anything going on inside either."

I checked my watch. We had an hour before we were to meet Matthieu. "Did the jeweler say when the trucks arrive?"

"She said it was difficult because they come and go at all hours for a few days. They wake her up when it starts, then a few days later it's all silent again."

"You got an awful lot of information. Are you sure it's safe to hang out here? That she hasn't called someone to say you were really interested in the warehouse?"

Lu laughed and motioned to the waiter. "Two glasses of wine, please. I didn't have to ask a lot of questions. I think she was just waiting for someone to listen to her complain. We're okay as long as she doesn't send us a real estate agent."

We watched the street while we sipped our wine, taking care to pay as much attention to the pedestrians as to the brown doors. "When we get back, I need to figure out that schedule. Maybe we can convince Matthieu to check into the warehouse if we can show him when the next trucks are going to come."

Lu paid the bill and we started walking back to the harbor. "What do you think the trucks are all about?" she asked.

"I guess some of them are bringing guns and some are taking them away." I looked at the street. "We didn't come this way, did we?"

"I don't remember that chocolate store and I think I would have. Look at the shapes. They make them so beautiful." She pulled at the door. "It's closed."

"We must have taken the wrong street on that first turn." I went to go back up to the cross street, but Lu pulled me back.

She pointed down the hill. "There's no guarantee we'll be able to find our way if we go back. Why don't we just keep going downhill? We'll get to the water eventually."

I figured we had plenty of time, so we worked our way downhill. It wasn't as straightforward as Lu made it sound. There were enough dead-end streets and wandering lanes that we took a half hour to get to the harbor, or rather to the water where we could see the harbor a mile away.

"I'm putting the GPS back in my purse," I said. "I don't care if it speaks randomly. I don't like getting lost."

"And I don't want to keep Matthieu waiting any longer," Lu said, marching toward the multicolored awnings.

NINE

Matthieu was talking to his cousin when we finally arrived, almost half an hour later than he expected us. "Ah, you must have been enjoying our small town."

Lu stepped a little closer to him and I gave the romance a boost by staying just a bit back. "We were exploring the streets above the harbor," she said. "There are so many small shops there."

"Yes. But you must come to the market tomorrow. The stalls line the streets around the center. You might find some interesting souvenirs. But I warn you, the parking will be atrocious."

He was much more relaxed outside the station. It was like he left a weight behind the door of his office. I hoped part of the difference was Lu. She blossomed when he was around. It was like a light went on when I didn't know it was off to start with. I felt like a terrible best friend for not noticing.

"We were planning to explore the market," Lu said. "We'll make sure we leave the car closer to the police station and then walk in."

"That is a perfect idea. I suggest you get there early. There are fresh croissants to be had. Perhaps you can take your breakfast here."

"Where are you taking us this evening, Matthieu?" I wasn't going to stand here all evening while they pretended not to be attracted to each other.

"I thought you might like to visit the fisherman's church. It is a small walk in this direction." He pointed the opposite way from where we'd been. "And I have obtained permission to show you the... hah but let that be a surprise."

Lu stepped closer still. If she took one more step, he was going to have to take her hand. But he just smiled, waved toward the church, and we were on our way. The street was wide enough for us to walk side by side, so I wasn't able to give Lu an opportunity to get closer to him without being obvious. As we walked, Matthieu entertained us with anecdotes about the people who had lived here in the past. "And of course, we have our share of celebrities who come here to get a rest from the paparazzi. But, enough of that, here we are."

He pointed to a small church on the water side of the street. In fact, it appeared to back right onto the Mediterranean. We crossed and went through the heavy double doors. Inside, the glow of the setting sun through small stained-glass windows gave the church a feeling of hushed respect. I admired the way churches were built. Somehow they felt inhabited even when they'd been empty for days. The inside of this one was bare stone floors and rough walls. The altar was simple, and instead of pews there were rows of collapsible chairs.

"Is the church still in use?" Lu asked.

We both stepped forward to look at the statues of saints that graced the side walls. It was much bigger inside, and I was right, it went to the water. I could hear a wet splash now and then.

Matthieu nodded. "Yes, there is a small congregation. Please notice the stained glass. It has survived many disasters. The locals think it is blessed and often ask a prayer to *La Sainte fée verte.*"

I looked at the pattern expecting to see a saintly portrait, but all I saw were patterns. It was like a vision through a Kaleido-scope, pretty, but no saint. "Who is *La Sainte fée verte*?"

"Well, she is not an official saint. The window was commissioned almost a hundred years ago, by a local distillery. They made absinthe." He pointed to the center of the floor where the sun painted the pattern on the stone. "You see, the color becomes green. And they say, if you are blessed, you can see the *Fée*, how do you say it? Ah, fairy."

I was skeptical, but Lu joined me in front of the light painting.

"I can see a shape in the middle, but I don't know if it is a fairy," Lu said and pointed to a black squiggle.

"Ah perhaps that is the fairy, but she is shy." Matthieu took Lu's elbow. "Come, I will show you the surprise."

I started planning how to give them alone time. I wasn't going to pass up a dinner with him, he was likely to come up with something spectacular, but maybe over dessert I could develop a headache and then Lu and he could spend the rest of the evening together. Then that glow I saw coming from Lu might continue after the holiday romance.

The surprise was down a narrow spiral stair. There was faint light at the bottom, and for a second I started to wonder if we were safe. Then Matthieu said, "There is a short corridor. At the end, please open the door but be careful, do not step through until I bring the lantern." He sounded like a little kid who was getting ready to show off a magic trick he'd learned. If the fairy wasn't the big surprise, I was eager to know what was.

Lu was ahead of me. She opened the door, and I felt a rush of damp and salty water. "The ocean is right there," she said.

The light grew as Matthieu approached, holding a lantern

lit by a single candle. If he ever got tired of being a gendarme, he had a great future in anything theatrical. We shifted and there was just enough room for the three of us in the doorway.

Matthieu held up the lantern and we saw the water rolling gently just past a small stone ledge. "This is the way that the old smugglers brought in their wares."

I looked carefully, but there was no evidence of any recent activity. "They brought the contraband through the church?" I pictured smugglers bending over caskets of wine and struggling up the stairs.

"No, but the church was how they came and went to the boats. Imagine two or three smugglers gathering where we are on these steps waiting for a boat to come down the tunnel. A boat that might take them away from France to avoid troubles, or one that might be filled with stolen jewels. Or perhaps one that was empty, ready to take wine from here to other ports where there were no taxes, or where officials were more willing to take bribes."

He painted a vivid picture of the times and I was lost for a few minutes in my imagination. I wonder if smuggling was ever as romantic as we think it was. My experience with it was far from the, not quite legal, adventure Matthieu was painting it.

"Matthieu, if they didn't bring the contraband through the church, where did they take it?" Lu sounded as entranced as I was.

"That is the next part of the surprise. Please be very careful, but if you step onto the ledge, you will find it wide enough to travel. Follow me."

He stepped out and moved to his left. Lu followed and I was right behind, not wanting to be left in the dark.

"So, here is the path that was taken to hide the spoils. Oh, yes, we had a few pirates here." He led us a few feet into a small room, almost a cave. "Now, you see that light?"

There was a faint glow coming through a small square patch in the ceiling.

"This is where the contraband was passed in or out of the boats. The doorway you see is in the middle of a kitchen across the street from the church. The goods would be gathered there, and then, when the time was right, dispersed to wherever the smugglers could get a profit."

"And they had to do that because they couldn't come through the church?" Lu voiced my question. "Why didn't they just arrange with the priest to use the church?"

"That is a very good question, Lu," Matthieu said. "It would probably have been easy to have the church made available, but why would they have any reason to be bringing goods back and forth through a church?"

Lu and I made noises of comprehension and then Matthieu said, "And, I sometimes think that criminals are attracted to complexity. Now, it is getting cold. We should leave and have our supper."

After another fabulous meal, I faked the headache so they could have some time alone. Matthieu put up a half-hearted protest but agreed to bring Lu home safely.

TEN

"It's been two days and we have nothing," Lu said, slamming the car door the next morning. "We need to do something."

"We haven't got nothing," I said. "We've found the probable storage location for the guns, or whatever they are smuggling. We have a working knowledge of the town, and we have a plan."

When she'd got in last night she was all cheerful and optimistic. She said they'd talked the whole time and yet, I noticed her lipstick was freshly applied. This morning, she was less optimistic and more rushed as we walked through the crowds toward the market.

"So, our plan is to pretend to shop in the market while we keep looking for suspicious activity and then have lunch near the warehouse." She made it sound stupid.

"You thought it was a good idea when we came up with it." If this was the effect Matthieu had on her, I was not leaving them alone again. "We figured if they take off when the market trucks go, they won't be as obvious."

She stopped on the corner and turned to look at me. "I know. You don't have to remind me what we thought."

I opened my mouth to speak, but she held up her hand. "I'm

sorry. I just don't like keeping things from Matthieu. I know we agreed to keep the notebook, but I think he would help us if we were honest with him."

That must have been some talking they did last night. I walked on and she followed. It felt like there were hundreds of people on the street, and when I turned the corner I saw why.

The harbor had changed into a maze of covered stalls. Awnings ranged from bright blue to sun faded yellow. Some of the stalls had their wares strung from wires twisted around the top of the supporting poles, some had barrels of olives, and sausage arranged in front. The nearest one was covered in cheeses, the next bread. Purses hung from a line on the third stall.

"Wow," Lu breathed. "Okay. I think we'll find plenty to keep us occupied until lunch."

"Let's get something to eat. Maybe you'll be in a better mood with some coffee and carbs in you." We found a pastry stall and stood munching on croissants until a couple of empty chairs opened up at the café next door. The town was buzzing with locals doing their regular shopping, and tourists wandering from stall to stall. We realized that it was unlikely that we'd see anyone skulking around in this crowd. "With this number of people, I'm more confident that they'll use the market to cover a delivery or a shipment."

Lu nodded. "I'm sorry I was grumpy this morning. I really do hate hiding things from Matthieu. I know it's crazy, but I want him to trust me. I feel like I need him to trust me."

"You are falling pretty fast." I didn't want to be a wet blanket. I liked seeing Lu feel a little passion, but it had been a long time since she'd dated anyone. Her husband's death had sent her into relationship hiding. Even after this long, she could be looking at some weird rebound romance. "Next time we talk to him, let me dig into this problem he has with his boss. It seems to me he's always throwing us the party line on the case. Maybe he doesn't agree with it. If that's true, he might help, regardless of whether we give him evidence or not."

"I'm seeing him tonight." She kept her eyes on the scarf she was thinking of buying. "We're going out for dinner again."

"Nice. And I guess I'm going to sit alone watching CSI in French?" I laughed. It would beat going over that notebook again. Last night I read it until my eyes bled. I got the idea of matching dates with markets at about midnight, just before Lu came in. There was a correlation between the two. Not every date in the notebook was a market date, but a good fifty percent were. "Is he picking you up at the house?"

"Yes, around six again. Why?" She always knew when I had an ulterior motive.

"We could give him the book and pictures then. Maybe when he comes in for a glass of wine, or better still, you can give them to him over dinner."

She finished buying the scarf and wrapped it around her neck as elegantly any of the other women in the crowd. "We'll do it when he comes in, so you'll be there." She must have seen me roll my eyes because she said, "I know, I'm a coward."

"No, you aren't. Anyway, let's find the tapenade stall, Reg told us about."

THE STALL REG described was halfway up the street leading to the warehouse. By the time we got there, Lu had bought two more scarves, and I was the proud owner of a tablecloth and six bars of olive oil soap.

The stall was busy, so we waited until there was a lull and then bought three small tubs of different olive spreads, and a bag of black, wrinkly, Nyons olives. "Thanks," I said taking the change. "Are you Guy? You were recommended by a friend. I can see why. You have such a wide selection."

"Yes, I am. And who was this wise person? I would like to make them a small gift the next time I see them." He smiled and winked at me.

Lu leaned forward to whisper, "Audrey Wylie. I know she loves your product."

"Yes, she buys from me every week. Except, last week, and today, is she perhaps on a holiday?" He put the tubs containing our purchases in a plastic bag and tied it off as we talked.

"We think she might be in trouble," I said quietly. "No one has seen her for a week and her house was ransacked." It was a risk telling him everything, but we needed to get information fast.

"I know nothing about that." He turned to the next customer, and then seemed to think better of it. "She was perhaps putting her nose into dangerous things."

We waited until there was another lull in his business, pretending to be interested in purses hanging on the stall next door. Okay, well since I bought one, it wasn't really pretending.

I got his attention by standing in front of him until he gave up pretending not to notice me. "I am trying to find her, and if you have any information you can give it to me. I won't tell anyone."

"Why would I worry about the gendarmes knowing?"

I cursed myself for slipping. "I thought perhaps your information would be damaging to Audrey, and you would want to protect her."

He considered this, glancing at people approaching his stall to make sure he wouldn't lose a sale. Finally, he sighed and asked, "Why would I believe you would help her if they have not?"

"Because the police aren't looking for her, and I am."

He blew a breath through his lips. "I will be taking a break in ten minutes. Go and get a table at that bar across the way. I will tell you what I know."

We waited at the bar, coffees in front of us while he sold to ten more customers before a woman came to take over the stall.

"Coffee," he called into the dark bar as he joined us. "I do not know exactly who she was investigating. But it was important to her. Do you know why she would do this?"

I couldn't really answer his question. Why didn't she just tell the police what she knew? I remembered Delores told us that they worked together in the civil rights movement. "Apparently, she was always protecting people."

He shrugged. "The last time I spoke to her, she said she was about to finish her investigation. She had some proof, she said, proof that would explain why criminals were able to work within the town."

"What do you mean?" I asked.

"There has always been a little crime here. You know the history?" He sipped the last of his coffee.

"We had a brief lesson yesterday." I wondered if Matthieu intended to tell us something other than a cute story last night.

"In the last few years, it has become something more than a little. There are some very nasty people here now." His gaze was on the stall. "I used to live here. I had a little shop where I sold the olives and oil and tapenade."

I had a feeling he wanted us to be interested, so I prodded a little. "What happened?"

"Someone wanted my shop. So, they put pressure on me. When that didn't work, they threatened my family, and my friends. Eventually I sold it and went on the road."

"Did you tell Audrey?" Lu asked.

"She knew me from the shop. And, yes, I did tell her. She said she missed coming to my place and I felt she needed to understand why we left. You know, it was really the best thing. My wife and I, we love traveling to the different towns. We should have done this years ago." He stood. "Thank you for the coffee. Now, ladies, I need to go back to my stall. Enjoy the market and good luck. Audrey was a nice lady."

"Where was your shop?" I asked, even though I had my suspicions.

"Just up the hill a little," he said, pointing in the direction of the warehouse.

ELEVEN

We didn't find anything else out so, eventually, we brought all our purchases back to the house. We ate lunch on the patio while we admired the things we'd bought at the market. At six o'clock the doorbell rang. Lu was still upstairs getting ready for her date, so I let Matthieu in. I figured she was dawdling just to make sure he had to join us for wine and evidence. "You look nice," I said as I checked out his suit. Gone was the elegant rumpled look. It was replaced with an elegant unrumpled black suit and pale blue shirt, no tie.

"Thank you, Charity." He looked around. "I see you have made the house livable again."

He was right, just having people live in the house seemed to erase the evidence of the break-in. "Lu will be down in a minute. Would you like a glass of wine?"

We'd decided to go with whatever his reaction was. The fridge had enough prepared food for dinner for all of us, if it took us a while to get and give information. If Matthieu made it easy, then I had dinner, and they had a date.

He sat on the couch and I poured three glasses. "Tell me,

Matthieu, why has the department decided that Audrey's case is closed?"

Before he could answer, Lu joined us. She was wearing a red dress that fit her like a second skin. That and the black heels were all it took to take Matthieu's attention away from me. He stood and she smiled, and it was like I didn't exist. It suddenly hit me that I was in danger of losing my best friend. The upside was I would always have a place to stay in France, but I'd miss her.

"Matthieu?" I said.

Lu sat and picked up her glass before he turned his attention back to me. "Ah, yes. The department sees no evidence of wrongdoing. That is why the case has been closed."

"What if we had new evidence?" I was willing to give him everything if he just came clean.

"The case has been discussed, and it seems all the evidence we have points to Audrey going on a holiday." He put down the glass and picked at the grapes and brie Lu had put out earlier.

"What do you think? I don't want the official word. I want to know what you think."

He looked at me and then at Lu. He took a sip of his wine, and then put the glass down. "It seems I must come clean as they say on the American television. I am not well liked, as you know, at the station."

Lu patted his knee and said, "Yes, we noticed."

He continued, "I do not agree that Madame Wylie is on holiday. I am unhappy with the way the Colonel is approaching the investigation. I should not say this, but I no longer care what my superiors think of me."

I looked at Lu. It was time for her to hand over our evidence. There was no way the book was in her purse. It was too small to hold anything more than a lipstick. And it was definitely not on her body; that dress didn't have pockets.

She put the wine glass down and said, "Tell him what Guy said. I'll be back."

I related what we'd learned from the tapenade guy, as I like to think of him. "So, you see, it's clear that she was on some trail. It's an unlikely coincidence that she would go on holiday right after telling Guy that."

"I did not know this," he said. "I would have followed up on that information."

"And yesterday we heard from a local businesswoman that trucks are moving something in and out of a warehouse near Guy's old store."

Lu returned with the notebook and pictures. "I am sorry, Matthieu. We were not sure that the police were serious about the investigation. We found these when we came to see the mess." She handed them to him.

"I should be arresting you for obstruction of an ongoing investigation," he said. "But since the investigation is closed, perhaps I can forgive you." He smiled. "Is there anything else you would like to tell me?"

We both shook our heads.

"What did you find in the book?" He settled back into the couch.

"The book has dates that we think relate to deliveries and shipments of guns. The pictures explain why. There are other notations, but we haven't figured them out."

"Is that all? Your snooping around town has not provided the vital clue?" I couldn't tell whether he was joking or not.

Lu answered, "We thought it had something to do with the market schedule. But we watched for a while today and no trucks came or went."

His head jerked up from the picture. "You watched? Where did you watch exactly? Is it possible someone saw you doing this watching?"

"The warehouse," I said. "Don't worry, no one saw us. We can show you." I looked at them and remembered they were supposed to be going on a date. "No, you go eat, and Lu can show you. Then come back and we'll talk about how to sort this out and find Audrey."

"I am not happy to leave you here, Charity. We do need to eat, yes. But please join us," Matthieu said.

I shook my head and said, "No, you didn't get dressed up to have dinner with me. Go eat, I'll be fine. I want to call Delores to tell her what's happening. And Jake emailed me. We've arranged to talk later."

They finally agreed and left me to the wine bottle, the food in the fridge, and my calls to Jake and Delores.

Seeing Lu that happy made me more homesick for Jake. I found myself impatient for the time when he would phone. I'd called him when we got the new phones, but we only had a few minutes available. The movie was a full-time job — twenty hours a day. It's not that I didn't feel happy for him that his career was picking up. I just wanted to talk to him and let him know how much I was looking forward to Paris.

I called Delores before I put my dinner together.

She asked the question I was dreading. "Charity, do you think Audrey is still alive?"

"I hope so," I said. "I know they haven't found a body."

Delores cleared her throat and said, "I hope you aren't keeping bad news from me. I expect you to be honest. If there is bad news, tell me."

I rolled my eyes and threw away my last preconception of Delores. From now on I would think of her as someone to get to know, someone interesting. "I have no reason to believe she's dead. Is she strong enough to survive a week as someone's captive?"

"She's older than I am, but she's healthy. Yes, I think as

long as she has food and water, she will be fine. In fact, she always had more backbone than I did. Audrey would never let go of a fight. I remember one time we were meeting with a school superintendent in Mississippi. He told her she should go home and tend to her husband." Delores laughed. "She told him that if he didn't listen to us, she would ensure that all he had to do with his day was go home and tend to his wife. The man just sat down and listened. It didn't change his opinion on segregation, but at least he listened."

That took a bit of weight off my shoulders. I had been worried that we would be a day too late when we did find her. "I'm sure we'll locate her soon. We have some help from the police now."

"Thank you for calling, Charity. I will let you go now. I know it's late there. Say hello to Lu."

I said goodbye and then made some notes for Matthieu on everything we'd figured out so far. I kept going until my phone finally chirped.

"Jake?" I said, and then smacked my forehead at the obvious statement. There were only two people who knew the number, and I didn't think Lu would be calling.

"Hey babe," he said in his sexy, leading man voice.

"Hey, how is the movie going?" I poured myself a little more wine.

"It's a real buzz. I am exhausted, but it's fun." I could hear people in the background, yelling and cheering.

"Are you going to have the energy for a week in Paris?" I planned to make the most of the time.

He shouted words I didn't catch at someone. "I'll rest up on the trip over there. Listen, Charity, I hate to do this, but I am going to be a day later than expected."

"But I miss you." I realized how petulant that was as the

words left my lips. "Sorry, I know it must be something important, or you wouldn't be late."

He didn't answer right away. My defenses slid into place. I shouldn't have let myself depend on him. There was something more important, or someone.

What felt like hours later, he said, "I have to take a meeting with the director of the movie we're shooting next. I told you it's back east, remember."

"And they can't do that in Paris? Or over the phone?" I took a gulp of wine.

"Charity, it's just a day. You and Lu can do the touristy things. It's not like I'm leaving you alone."

I wasn't going to tell him that Lu might not be in Paris. I didn't need his pity. "Fine."

"Babe, come on. I promise, I'll make it up to you. What are the two of you doing with your time anyway?" His quick change of the subject was probably wise.

"We're staying in a friend of Delores' house. Uh, she's missing and we're trying to help the police find her." Well, sort of the truth. "You know, we're right on the Mediterranean, you could come here instead of Paris."

"You are investigating while on vacation. And you want to buy some time. So, me being a day late isn't all that much of a problem." He was too smart by half.

"I do miss you, and I am looking forward to Paris. I think we should talk." If he could try to make this my problem, I could play dirty too. "About our relationship."

The noise at his end rose and fell, and then it was suddenly very quiet. "What about our relationship? I thought you were happy with it the way it was."

"What's going on there? Were you at a party?" I tried not to feel too good about putting him off his attack.

"No, we're watching a hockey game. I stepped outside." He

waited then, when I didn't respond, he asked, "Are you breaking up with me over a day in Paris?"

"No, I meant—"

"Charity, I can't believe you are that angry about one day. Especially since you're involved in an investigation."

"Jake, I'm not breaking up with you. Why did you think that?" This was so far off track I wanted to hang up and start again.

"Because you are always finding an excuse to push me away, because you made it very clear that you don't want to get any deeper into the relationship."

I sipped more wine, realizing it wasn't helping my judgment, but needing something to stop me blurting out exactly what he expected of me. "Wait, let's talk about something else. I am not breaking up with you. I'm not having a relationship discussion on a phone."

"Fine." He sighed with the word. "How is your investigation going?"

I told him about the clues we'd found and about the way the police were treating the case as closed.

"I have confidence in you," he said. "Just don't go getting yourself hurt. We have a relationship conversation to get through in a few days."

"I promise. Anyway, I don't think Matthieu will let us get into any trouble."

"Who's Matthieu?" *Did I hear a twinge of jealousy in his voice?*

"He's the cop we're working with. Well, I think we'll start working with him later tonight."

"You have a man coming there tonight? Should I be worried?" He said it as a joke, but I definitely heard jealousy.

"Well you should be if you were thinking of hooking up

with Lu. They are in the throes of a holiday romance." I chuckled at his overacted gasp.

"Our Lu? The one I thought took vows of celibacy?"

"Yep. I'm not sure the celibacy thing has changed, but you never know. They're out on a date right now."

We gossiped for a while about what Lu and Matthieu might be up to and then said goodbye. I was glad we'd gotten past the start of the fight. We would usually go from start to irate in seconds. It was hard to keep perspective with him working so far away. I didn't want to lose him because of a misunderstanding.

TWELVE

An hour after I hung up with Jake, Matthieu and Lu came back. They were holding hands and I marveled at the speed at which they had settled into this relationship. Lu took years to get ready to fall in love, but when she did it was all in. I'd taken years with Jake to realize maybe I was in love.

"Coffee?" I called from the kitchen.

"No, thanks. I'm not sure I will get any sleep if I have another cup," Lu answered. "But if there's a bottle of wine..."

Matthieu asked for tea, and I put the kettle on. I joined Lu with wine. I could dry out my liver when we got home. "So, did you have a nice dinner?"

"It was delicious," she answered. "Matthieu knows so many of the chefs in town. We ate at different restaurants for each course, and he knew just the right choice."

"It is simple to know what to order. You are very easily pleased, Lu." He took the cup and teapot to the living room. "Now the enjoyable part of the evening is, possibly, over. It is time to see this evidence. Tell me again where you found them?"

Lu explained how she'd found both items. "But there's

nothing more. We've knocked and tapped every possible surface."

"I will have to take these to the Colonel. Perhaps he will reopen the case." He sighed, "Ah, I do not believe that. I think there is... no. I must take it in."

"What if you helped us find out what's going on?" Lu asked. "I mean, we've given it to the police, technically."

"I have been ordered to leave the case alone." He started flipping through the book. "I may not agree with the orders, but I must follow them. But, tonight, let us just talk about what you have found. If it is enough to change the mind of the Colonel, perhaps we can reopen the case."

I gave him my notes. "Did you manage to wander by the warehouse we found?"

"We did find ourselves in the neighborhood. It is a location that is, as you say, known to the police." He flipped through my notes and nodded. "Your analysis of the dates is very good. And your conversation with Guy Malmont seems to support your suspicions."

In the meantime, Audrey stays missing. "We need to ramp up this investigation, Matthieu," I said. "If you take the book and pictures into the station and they won't reopen the case, we'll lose more time. We need your knowledge of the town to go further. Please don't just dump this back in the system."

"If I do not inform the Colonel, it will be difficult to proceed."

"If you do, and he doesn't reopen the case, we've lost our only clues." I could feel my cheeks starting to heat with anger.

"Charity, it's not his fault," Lu said and then turned back to him. "There must be some solution, Matthieu." Lu's voice had lost the glow of love and gained the chill of exasperation. "What would happen if you helped us?"

"I would be suspended, which means I will have more time

to spend with you before you leave, but it does not mean I will be able to help you."

"What would it take?" she asked.

"I have not yet been ordered to not help you. If I were not available to hear that, perhaps I can help. I have a few days of vacation that I can schedule. I will call tomorrow and arrange a leave for the rest of the week."

Lu beamed at him and said, "Thank you, Matthieu. I know this will cause you problems when you return to work."

He waved off her thanks. "I will only get into trouble if we do not find Madame Wylie."

That was good, but there was still something going on. "Matthieu, what were you going to say earlier?"

He avoided looking at me. "When?"

"When you said, 'I think there is'. You think there is what?"

"Charity, I was going to be indiscreet, but I will not do so. Now I suggest we look closely at this information because I will have to leave soon. And when I do, I will need to take them with me."

"And will you take them into the station?" Lu voiced the question I was thinking. If he was going to take time off to help, did that mean he was going keep our progress outside the office, too?

"I don't know how long it will work," he said. "But I will need to keep these for a while." He frowned at both of us. "And that means I will hold them, not we."

TWO HOURS LATER, Matthieu rubbed his eyes and said, "It would be easier if I had access to my computer. I think I have found something, but I need to check it out."

"Is it something we could research from here? There is a

laptop and a wireless network somewhere in the neighborhood."
I'd checked it out earlier in the day.

"No. I need to access the system from work. Apparently, our
computers are behind a barrier. This information is also behind
it, and I do not know how to bypass the security. Perhaps I will
do a little work tomorrow before I start my vacation." He
yawned, politely. "I apologize. It has been a long day."

Lu had curled up on the corner of the couch ten minutes
ago, and I was having trouble keeping my eyes open. I managed
to force some energy into my voice. "What do you think you
found?"

"Perhaps found is not the right expression. Something was
prompted by what I read. Madame Wylie was diligent in noting
dates and times. I think you are right. Some of them are market
days. But I think also some of them might be related to tides and
boats."

Light dawned. "So, if we knew the tide schedule, we might
see a pattern. That, we can get through Google." How had I
missed such a regular pattern?

"That is not the hard part," he said, while gathering the
notes, pictures, and book together. "I could probably work out
that schedule in my head. The information I need from the official network is the ownership of the boats. If I know that, I can
track boats across the ports."

"Okay. I guess you should go before you fall asleep." I
stretched and heard a lot of popping and snapping. "Or until I
fall asleep like Lu."

"I will be back in the morning." He stood and stuffed the
papers into his pockets. "I will only need an hour on the system.
I still do the job the old-fashioned way. Often my colleagues
believe the computer can solve crimes. I believe it is a good tool,
but not the whole solution."

Lu woke up as Matthieu bent to kiss her cheek. I swear it

was starting to look more like I was going to be visiting her here, rather than just across the Lion's Gate Bridge. They became more like an old married couple as time passed.

"Let me walk you to the door," she said as she uncurled.

"I'll leave you to it. See you in the morning, Matthieu." I went upstairs because I couldn't watch them together any longer. The more I saw them, the more I missed Jake.

THIRTEEN

I was making coffee the next morning and it was odd to be alone. Lu, usually up before me, was sleeping in and Matthieu wasn't due for an hour or so. When the coffee was dripping, I put bread, butter, and jam on a platter so we could eat on the patio – a bit chilly but doable. It seemed we were here at a perfect time, before the heat started baking and after the chill of winter.

I'd brought a bowl of fruit out already, and I took the platter out with a handful of cutlery to join it.

"*Bonjour*," a voice called over the stone wall. It was the neighbor who we'd missed yesterday.

I walked over to the wall and stood on a bench that had been placed there so people could watch the sunset. "*Bonjour*," I said to the little lady who was standing on tiptoes in her own yard.

"Ah English," she said. I had learned that meant language not nationality, so I didn't correct her. "Monsieur Black said you were asking about Audrey, yes?"

"Yes. We are trying to find her."

"Ah, yes, the gendarme said so when he told me you would

be living in the house. It is terrible that someone should just disappear." She fanned herself at the shock of it.

"Would you like to join me for coffee? It will be better than us talking over the wall."

She nodded and dashed back into her house. I brought out cups, milk, and sugar while she made her way over.

"Thank you. I am Madame Lesart. You may call me Claudette." She held out a small bottle. "Please, I make this, and I think you may enjoy it."

"Thank you, my name is Charity Deacon. Of course you can call me Charity." I took the bottle and saw it contained a dark liquid. "What is this?" I gestured for her to sit.

"A little thing that I make for friends. It is for, how do you say..." She frowned as she dug for the word. "Ah, for the digestion. To drink before a meal. It is a family recipe for *Pastis*."

I had no idea people were allowed to make distilled alcohol here. Much more civilized than home. "Thank you, I'm sure we will enjoy it tonight. I hope we'll be able to share it with Audrey soon."

I poured the coffee and she stirred in three heaping spoons of sugar. What was it with the French and sugar?

Claudette took a sip and smiled. I gestured to the food, and she shook her head. "Oh no, *merci*. I have already eaten. I wanted to tell you that I may have some information for you. The gendarme who came did not seem interested, but perhaps you are?"

Any source of information was welcome, and I'd make sure Matthieu heard about the lack of interest she'd encountered. I nodded and it was like taking the top off a shaken beer. She started talking, "Well, before Audrey went missing, she had a visitor. I saw from the window upstairs." She pointed to a window that overlooked the front of Audrey's house. "I did not intend to snoop, as you say, but the woman came into the garden here." She pointed to the gate. "She was unusual as a visitor for my friend."

She stopped. I assumed to take a breath because I didn't get a chance to ask her anything before she continued, "This woman was very thin and her hair, well it was the most unusual shade of red. Like rust, like the women in Paris used to wear it. But not so elegant. Hers was all in disarray and spiky, very short."

I nodded as though agreeing how terrible it was that a woman would allow herself to get into such a state.

"Well, she approached the door, and Audrey must have known she was there because the door opened without her having to knock. It is odd, yes?"

"Yes," I said and refilled her cup, although she was, perhaps, already over caffeinated. I had to force myself not to look up at the window. But if I remembered correctly, to see all this action, Claudette must have been half hanging out of it.

"Thank you," she said, stirring more sugar in. "Perhaps I will have a small croissant."

I waited while she placed the pastry on a plate and added a spoonful of marmalade.

"Most delicious," she said after taking a dainty bite. "Now, I would normally do my best to ignore what I heard next, but it was impossible. The woman shouted at Audrey that she should stay away from them, that she would regret the day she did not. That he would punish Audrey." She nodded as though to punctuate her words with authority and took another bite of the pastry.

"Do you know who she meant by he? Did a man come with the woman?" I asked, trying to take advantage of the fact she was eating.

"Oh, my dear, no. I am certain that the woman was alone.

Audrey said that she was not afraid, and that it was very wrong what he was doing." Claudette took another nip at the croissant.

"Then what happened?"

"Ah, the woman marched out of the house and left. Then the next evening I saw the car again. And then yesterday, I am told my dear friend has been missing for days."

I wished I had a notebook. Writing out what Claudette was saying would help me remember it, and maybe help me make connections. "Can you describe the car?"

"To me all cars are very much the same. My dear husband would have known exactly what type of car it was. But he passed many years ago."

"Was it big? Dark? New?" I was probably going to have to get Matthieu to talk to her, but I wanted to get as much information as possible. And, I had to admit, she was very entertaining.

"It looked rich, like those horrible German cars that everyone seems to want. Dark, yes. Perhaps it was green or blue?" She finished her coffee and croissant. "This will help you, yes?"

"It will. Thank you for telling me. I may ask a friend in the police department to speak to you, would that be okay?"

"This friend, it is Matthieu Durand, yes?" She gave a sweet little smile as she said his name.

"How did you know?"

"I have seen him come and go since you girls have been staying at Audrey's. I see the way he is with your friend." She raised an eyebrow.

"Her name is Luscious Cho. You can call her Lu when you see her."

"Lu, an odd name for such a lovely lady. Ah, but never mind. I think it is well past the time when Matthieu settled down again. He is a good boy. Now I must be going. You can have Matthieu come to my house if he wishes."

She stood and hurried through the garden back to her house. I was left wondering if Lu knew that Matthieu had once settled down with someone, and if it would even matter to her.

"WHO WERE YOU TALKING TO?" Lu asked as she joined me on the patio a half hour later. Today she wore a cream-colored, heavy sweater over plum trousers. I was dressed in my usual jeans with a brightly colored scarf over my white tee-shirt. Maybe I should start dressing more like Lu and less like an over-aged teen.

"The neighbor," I said then brought her up to date as we shared breakfast.

"It seems you've found another Delores," she said before going into the kitchen to start another pot of coffee.

When she came back with a clean cup for Matthieu, I asked, "What do you mean another Delores?"

"Nosy neighbor."

I laughed. "You know I was so caught up in how cute she was I didn't give much thought to it."

I remembered my image of Claudette hanging out of her window to see what was going on. I couldn't see Delores doing that. It wouldn't be proper. But I guess it was nice to have a neighbor who cared. "She seems way more fun than Delores anyway."

"True. Let's hope her information helps. I'm dying to meet this Audrey. Someone who could be best friends with two such different women is bound to be interesting." Lu waved to Matthieu who had just come in the gate. "Get yourself some breakfast," she said. Then she went to retrieve the fresh coffee while Matthieu settled in the chair Claudette had vacated.

When we were all sitting around the table, I glanced up to make sure Claudette wasn't watching. The window was empty.

Although I guess she could be anywhere behind the garden wall.

"Did you find anything?" I asked, not wanting to tell the story again until we knew more about the information in the notebook.

"I did. I was correct that there were matches with the tides. I have two particular boats that were out on the ocean almost every date recorded. I couldn't stay any longer without raising suspicion since I was going to be on holiday." He grinned and waved his hand down the blue golf shirt and khaki pants. "You see I am in casual clothes."

Yes, he was. It's just that the khakis looked newly pressed and the golf shirt was definitely not polyester blend. It looked more like silk. I was actually going to have to get some fashion sense to fit in.

"So, the next steps are to figure out who was on the boats?" Lu asked.

"*Oui*, yes. I have a friend in the harbor master's office who will be able to give us that information. We should go soon."

I nodded and said, "I have something too. I had a visitor this morning." I gave him all the details but in a more ordered manner than Claudette; the girl, car, the argument, the car coming back. I left out her comments on Lu's suitability as a mate.

"I know Claudette very well. She was a great friend of my mother's and she introduced me to my first wife."

Lu didn't react to that, so it seemed she knew about it. I'd get any gossip later. As he said, we needed to get going. If we worked all day and were lucky, we might find Audrey.

"Did Claudette mention that this mystery woman had a limp?" He glanced at the house next door as he asked. "There are many women who are skinny here, and anyone can dye their hair."

"No," I followed his gaze. "I think she's still there. At least, she hasn't come out the front door, maybe there's a back way out?"

"Most houses here do not have exits from the back garden. Let me go and ask." He rose. "I will not be gone as long this time. We can go to the harbor when I get back."

As soon as he was invited into Claudette's house I turned to Lu. "Not as long this time?"

She blushed. "I guess you must have been really tired last night."

I rolled my eyes. "And when did you know about the other wife?"

"Don't say it that way. She died ten years ago. Cancer." Lu barely managed the last words.

"Sorry, I didn't mean to be flip." I really hadn't meant to upset her. I guess I was more used to a relationship that was underscored by bickering. Having one that relied on conversation and openness seemed weird.

"No, you couldn't have known. But he told me over dinner. We told each other everything." She looked across at the house. "This isn't a holiday romance, Charity."

"I guessed that. So, have you talked about where you'll live?" I tried to sound light, but my best friend was leaving me. I know it's childish, but I didn't want to lose her.

She slapped my arm lightly and said, "Don't worry, I'm not deserting you. We haven't talked about it, at least not yet."

We both laughed. I would get over it, and I did really want her to be happy.

Matthieu returned after about five minutes. "It seems our mystery woman did have a limp. I think we have a new lead, a very good new lead. She is someone we know. A lot of petty crime when she was a child. Now she is low in the local crime organization. Or that is what we believed." Matthieu carried the empty tray inside.

"So, what does that mean? Or so you believed?" I had the feeling there was something important Matthieu was holding back.

"We need to go start our search," he said. "I cannot tell you all the details, but we were planning to use Odette Pilon as our way into the higher levels of the organization. We believed we were going to break the gang. Perhaps only a small respite in the ongoing battle, but she would have been important."

Lu and I were gathering our purses and various other pieces of equipment. I looked up at Matthieu who was waiting patiently – or at least that's what it looked like. "So now you think she's part of the organization. Higher up?"

"Her car is an old Peugeot, not something that would be described as rich, or German, by anyone who is able to see. She appears to be the last one to see Madame Wylie before she disappeared. And, according to Claudette, she was confident in her assertion that she had the ability to call someone with power."

We locked the door and walked to Matthieu's car "What kind of things did she get into trouble about as a kid?" I was wondering if we could use some leverage if we met her.

"She has a temper. She stole some things. There are two assault charges. We knew her family. This is a small town for some people. Families know each other and don't change from generation to generation. When she was young, we... I think you say we cut her some slack. Her father was in jail more than he was at home. Her mother had to make money whatever way she could. Sometimes we had to ignore what she was doing. Odette needed one parent, no matter what that parent did."

Matthieu and Lu sat beside each other in the front of the car and I sat in the back. Leaning forward I said, "Okay so what are we going to do first? The harbor master, or this Odette?"

Matthieu turned the car toward the harbor. "We will do both this morning, but I know where we will find Odette now. And I know where we will find my friend all day."

"Matthieu, dear," Lu said, her voice gentle. "You are being cryptic. Tell us what you are planning, and we will help. I promise we will. But if you don't tell us plainly, we can't help, and might get in the way."

"Ah, I am sorry. I am so used to speaking with my colleagues." He focused on the traffic for a few moments. "Now, we will find Odette at home. She has to be there to ensure her mother eats at least one meal. The woman is dying."

"Oh, that's sad," Lu said.

"Yes. Unfortunately, she became addicted to drugs – heroin. Addiction was going to kill her in the long run, but AIDS will kill her first. But do not feel sorry for Odette. One of the things she has taken on as part of the criminal world is drug dealing."

"So, she's responsible for her mother's addiction?" No one needed to see their mother die of a horrible disease, but if Odette was dealing, she was causing the heartache in more families than her own.

"No, but it is something she feels deeply. I think she hates her mother for being so weak. But she loves her mother for the sacrifices she made."

I could understand that. One of the things that I hated about my parents' dying so far away from me was that they were helping everyone else. I guessed the flip side of this Odette's problem.

"So, what are we going to do when we get there?" I asked

Matthieu kept his eyes on the road. "I think you would be safer staying in the car. I will tell you what I learn."

"I'm not sitting in the car waiting for you to get the answers," I said.

Matthieu concentrated on making a turn. I got the feeling he was stalling for time.

"Matthieu," Lu said when the car was on a straight stretch of road. "We did not ask you to take over the investigation. We asked you to help. Please don't make this hard."

He sighed. "When we see her, please let me do the talking. I would much prefer you to both stay in the car. But I understand that is impossible. Let me deal with Odette, I know her. And she is volatile and dangerous."

"Do you want us to do anything? I am not going to just stand there." I realize that sounded churlish. "I mean, what can we do to help?"

"I am used to working with gendarmes. I know all of their skills. Tell me what you think you might do to contribute." He pulled up in a tight parking space in a part of the harbor that we'd missed. On this street, the doors were close together, giving the impression of thin slices of homes behind.

"It would help if you conducted this interview in English. We could be someone she wanted to impress. Or, I guess, if she would want to impress someone, we could play that role," I said.

"Good idea. She sees herself as important and informed. If you were more European, we could introduce you as Interpol."

"Would she be impressed with the CIA?" Lu asked. I knew she was my best friend for some reason.

"Yes. In fact, that would make her feel very important." He pointed and said, "That's her mother's home. Are you intending to be CIA operatives? What would be the reason you are here?"

"Not CIA," I said. I was pretty sure there would be some major repercussions if we pretended to be that. "What if we left it up to her imagination? We are from an international organization. Let her fill in the gaps."

"Very well. I will introduce you in English. That should be enough. I'll let her assume you are official."

We'd parked at the bottom of a street that wound uphill in twists and turns. It was on the edge of the old town, and what I could see of the street, alternated between store windows and what looked like doors to homes. The windows of the storefronts were grimy and clearly not looking for tourist trade. There was a slight taint of rotting fish in the air.

"This is as close as we can get by car. As you can see, the roadway is narrow and there are restrictions on parking that even we gendarmes have to obey." Matthieu opened the door for Lu and then the back one for me before opening the trunk and digging into a box. "I think we will look more official if you have these."

I expected guns, well, not really but I didn't know what else to expect. Then he handed both of us folders filled with sheets of paper. I looked through the papers and saw notes and official looking letterhead. "Good disguise as along as she doesn't ask for our ID."

"It won't be a problem. Just let me take the lead. Stay a little behind me and look stern if possible." He straightened his jacket, told me to stand tall, and led us up the hill.

We were two turns up the twisted street when Matthieu stopped in front of a weather-beaten pink door and rapped the iron ring. "It may take some time for her to open the door. I am told she rarely rises this early."

We waited a few minutes while Lu and I kept our faces stern. Well, hers looked stern to me, but mine felt more stiff than stern. Matthieu knocked again, this time longer than before. "Mademoiselle Pilon, it is the police."

After another few minutes, we heard a bolt side then the door opened, and a woman stared at Matthieu with a mixture of anger and sulk on her face. She lounged against the door frame, and I saw what Claudette meant about her hair. First of all, it made her skin look greenish, and second it was damaged into the consistency of hay. Rust colored hay.

"I am Lieutenant Durand. These are my colleagues."

"I know who you are, Durand." Her voice was harsh. She reached into a pocket and pulled out an unfiltered cigarette and plastic lighter. "Why are we speaking English? Don't your friends from Interpol understand French?"

"I would like to discuss this inside," he said.

"Sure, I let you in and you plant some evidence in my house." She took a deep drag on the cigarette then spat tobacco from her lip. "What do you want?"

"I think you would prefer that we do this inside," Lu said. Her voice was all official and cold. "I do not think your neighbors need to hear what we want to ask? Or perhaps they don't want to hear the answers you will give."

I got the feeling she'd use whatever methods were necessary to get the answers. My best buddy should think about an acting career. Odette drew on the cigarette again as she gave Lu the up and down stare. Then she shrugged and turned to walk back into the dim hall. Matthieu followed her, Lu right behind him. I looked around the street before stepping after them and pulling the door closed behind us.

We ended up in a kitchen at the back of the house. There was a large window and a door to the courtyard. The door stood open, and I could smell lavender and thyme. The kitchen was tidy even though it was worn. A well-used, but sturdy, table and chairs filled most of the space.

"Ask your questions. I have places to be." She leaned against the wall, and I wondered if she ever sat down.

Matthieu took a notebook out of his pocket and flipped though some of the pages as though to review his notes. "We have a report that you were seen threatening a woman just before she disappeared."

"I don't remember threatening any old ladies lately." She stubbed out her cigarette in a saucer.

I opened my folder and made a note. When I looked up, she was staring at me. I smiled back and closed the folder. Matthieu didn't comment on her 'old ladies' addition to his accusation.

"Madame Audrey Wylie," Matthieu said. "She lives in the suburbs south, in a neighborhood where people look out for each other."

"I still do not know this woman. Wylie, what kind of name is that?"

Matthieu seemed to consider for a moment. "She is Canadian. Her friends there have reported her missing. I would like to ensure we resolve this without the aid of the international authorities." He glanced at me as he said the last words. *Nice going, Matthieu.*

I made another note and hmmed. Lu looked carefully at Odette then leaned in to whisper in my ear. I nodded.

"What makes you think the outsiders will find out anything in this town? If you can't find this woman, I don't see why we should worry about others coming in." She fumbled for another cigarette, her hand shaking as she lit it.

Matthieu stared at her and finally said, "How do you explain the fact that you were seen at her house?"

She shrugged. "I have that look. I'm often mistaken for someone else."

I raised an eyebrow but kept my mouth shut. I was going for the strong silent type.

Matthieu just waited.

She looked out of the window. "If I was there, then she was at home when I left. Did the nosy neighbors tell you this?"

"We have reason to believe you were not alone, or that you came back with someone. I can take you to the station where we can continue this discussion if you wish." Matthieu's voice remained calm. I would have to remember that technique. It was discomforting to me just listening to him ask questions with no emotion behind them. It must be what was shaking Odette up.

She flicked some ash off the cigarette. "I was under the impression that the case was closed. Are you sure no one will mind if you continue to pursue this? Perhaps it is time for you to leave, before things become too... well, before it becomes impossible to undo your actions."

Matthieu glanced at his watch and nodded. "Yes, it is time we were going to the next meeting." He flicked his hand toward the corridor and Lu led us out. Odette stayed in the kitchen. I heard the lighter click again as she lit the third cigarette.

FOURTEEN

The next stop was to meet the harbor master, Jean-Luc Fournier. His office was a small room facing the harbor. The walls were covered with pictures of boats, all different pictures, from posters of luxury liners of the twenties, to printouts of snapshots of the boats I could see across the street.

"Ah, Matthieu, I hear you are taking a vacation. I cannot blame you if it means you spend your day with lovely ladies like these." He grinned and held out his hand.

Matthieu introduced us and Jean-Luc kissed our hands then our cheeks. "Lovely ladies."

"Maybe I should tell Marie how lovely you think the ladies are?" Matthieu laughed as he said it, but there was an undertone of warning in his eyes. And he stepped a little closer to Lu.

Jean-Luc sighed. "Ah, perhaps that would not be a good idea. Can I offer you coffee?" He turned to a small espresso machine.

When we were sitting on stools clustered around his desk with tiny coffee cups in hand, Jean-Luc turned to Matthieu. "So, this vacation. I know you. It is not for rest or relaxation. You are, again, pursuing something that the Colonel has determined is not worthy of the time of the gendarmerie."

"We are following some unofficial leads in the Audrey Wylie case. I would prefer it if you could keep it discreet. It would be difficult if the Colonel were to decide to pay attention. It might..." He shrugged.

Jean-Luc sipped his coffee. "If he hears about it, it will not be from me. What can I do to help? Audrey was a good lady; she helped my Marie find her sister. You remember. We found out that she had a sister who was adopted."

"I remember, *mon ami*," Matthieu said as he pulled the notebook from his pocket. "We found this information. I want you to look at the dates and times. I think you might know more than I about the boat movements."

Jean-Luc took the book and flipped through the pages. "You have already noticed the boats that are involved. These dates you have circled? They seem very regular. Let me check." He shoved a stack of papers to the side and revealed a laptop on the center of his desk.

He muttered what sounded like encouraging words as he booted up the laptop and started banging on the keyboard. A few minutes later he said, "It is as I suspected. Look." He turned the laptop around, and I saw a list of dates and one name attached to each. The column header on the name was *bateau de pêche*.

Matthieu raised an eyebrow and said, "*Le Canard Bleu*. Marran's boat."

"You had already guessed, yes?" Jean-Luc went to the wall and took down a photograph. "Ladies, this is what the boat looks like. Matthieu knows we have searched it so many times I know it like my own home, better even. We know there is some way that he is smuggling. We cannot prove anything, yet."

"We have not always cared so much," Matthieu said. "We

used to intercept his boat looking for cigarettes and wine, and some designer jewelry. But now, I think he is greedy, and making dangerous alliances."

"Let us hope we can capture him before this goes too far." Jean-Luc sounded pessimistic.

I looked at the list, only Marran's boat showed. "How did you query the data?" They all turned from the screen to me. "I mean, it seems very odd to me that only his boat matches those dates. This is a working harbor, so boats are coming in all the time."

"Yes, a very good observation, Charity." Jean-Luc turned the laptop around again. "I was working on an assumption with my first request. I had planned to look at it in other ways." He stopped typing and turned the laptop to face us again. "See, when I ask to plot it by the time, it is always off the tide. Just a little, but enough."

The screen now showed a graph, *Le Canard Bleu* was indicated by a line of bright yellow dots. Two other boats were highlighted in red and blue, but all the others were just black. The black dots formed a tight wave across the graph. "Is this based on the tide?" I pointed at the wave of black, and Jean-Luc nodded. "So, the colored dots are almost always just behind or just ahead of the tide?"

Lu tapped the screen with a fingertip. "Mostly behind. They leave just after the rest of the boats," she said. "Look, even when they go out with the rest, it's at the edge of the timeline."

Matthieu sighed. "This is going to be difficult. I think he will be expecting us, and once again we will be obstructed."

I turned my attention back to the screen. It really nagged at me, all this data and it couldn't help us. "What are the other two boats? The blue and red dots?"

"These boats are owned by Marran's brother and his business partner." Jean-Luc cleared the screen of everything but the colored dots. "See, they don't have a pattern. I find that very odd, no?"

"Is there any way I can have access to the data?" I'd been taking lessons in data mining because that's what a good PI did, look through information. I figured if I could play around with the information, I could make a connection.

Jean-Lu shrugged, that really expressive movement, the one that includes everything from the top of his head through his upper body. "I cannot give you a copy, but I can give you access. You cannot let anyone know about this," he said, looking directly into my eyes. "I will create a secondary password for myself. I will explain that I sometimes need to access information through an unsecured network."

He turned the laptop, and after a few clicks wrote on a piece of paper. "Here is your user name and password. You will need to change the password the first time you log on."

I thanked him and started thinking about what I would be doing when I could spend some time with the data.

Matthieu looked at his watch and said, "We must go. According to this computer, Marran is out on the boat. We need to eat if we are going to speak to him when he gets back. We have two or three hours depending how long behind the tide he comes."

WE SAT in the shade of a bright green Perrier umbrella with two pizzas and a plate of *charcuterie* in front of us. Sharing all the plates solved our inability to decide, without wasting food.

I'd come up with a plan for analyzing the data while we waited for our lunch. "I'm going to try to build relationships between Marran's boats and the others. If there's a time stamp and we know where the fish are supposed to be, I should be able to build a picture of the route everyone is taking." I picked a slice of sausage off the plate. It was chewy, and tangy, and savory. I closed my eyes to try to imprint the memory. "I need time to concentrate on the data. What's the plan for the rest of the day?"

Matthieu wiped the condensation off his glass of beer and took a sip before answering, "I have been thinking about how we approach Marran. I cannot do so in an official capacity. I would be surprised if he didn't already know I was on leave."

"Would he talk to a tourist?" Lu asked. "I could bump into him, casually and—"

Matthieu and I both said no. I added, "He is not some television villain."

Matthieu continued my thought, "I do not want either of you in danger. We will just talk to him. And, when I say 'we', I mean me. You will wait here, or you will go shopping."

"Matthieu," Lu said, her voice chilled. "We will not go shopping like good little girls. I intend to be there. I'm sure Charity will not miss out on this interview either."

"He is a very dangerous man." Matthieu's voice was gentle. "It would be better that he did not know you were involved. I gave in to your wishes with Odette Pilon, but I am adamant that I will not allow you to be in danger here."

Lu was mad. I could see it in the ice forming between her and Matthieu. I said, "I think we're probably too late for that. Everyone seems to know everyone's business here."

Matthieu didn't meet my eyes. "It is possible, and you right. If he doesn't know now, Odette will tell him as soon as she can. I would like to take advantage of the small time between him arriving and her finding him."

I glared at Lu to tell her I would take care of it, before saying, "Sure, I can see why you want to do that. I think we should use the time to plan our data queries." I pasted a wide grin on my face.

Lu defrosted a bit. "Maybe we can have the paper folders back from the car. We'll need something to make notes on." If Matthieu had known us better, he would have been on his guard.

He gave us a look that said, *I know there's something going on here, but I'll let you get away with it for now.* I revised my estimate of how well he knew us. It was hard to remember he was a cop when we were sitting in a cafe looking out over the harbor of a quaint French town, the sun flickering off the waves in the distance.

My phone rang before I said something to tip him off. "It's Jake. I'll just take it over there." I pointed to a bench across the street. "Won't be long." I left feeling a little guilty that I was abandoning Lu to keep the lies afloat.

FIFTEEN

When I got back to the restaurant, Lu and Matthieu were heading for the entrance. I waited for them to join me on the sidewalk. "So what now?" I asked.

Matthieu gestured to the car. "I have conceded the point. We go to see Arnaud Marran. He lives at the top of the hill. We can get close by car, but we will have to walk a short distance."

I winked at Lu, and she grinned back. I'm sure Matthieu would learn pretty quickly how to make his 'no' stick, but until then, we were involved.

We were settled in the car before I had a chance to ask any questions, so they came out in a rush. "What's the exact plan? Do we interrogate him? Do you have any leverage we can use? Does every criminal live at the top of a hill where we have to approach on foot?"

Matthieu laughed. "Are you finished? Can I answer your questions before you start asking more?"

"I'm sorry. I guess I want this done so I can get to Paris."

Lu turned to smile at me. "The call must have been good. No arguments?"

Is that how she saw our relationship? Jake and I stumbling

from argument to argument? "No, we've both turned over a new leaf. No more fighting over things we can't change. I seem to have a role model now."

Matthieu chuckled. "Do not stop arguing completely, it is not healthy to stifle disagreements. To answer your questions, yes, a number of our criminal element live in this district. As you have noticed, it is much more difficult to launch an attack on any house up the hill. So, that means the criminals naturally gravitate to this area. Do not worry. We can launch an attack, but since it is the three of us only, our attack will be less visible, yes?"

"Ah, the heroic trio," Lu said. "Let's hope there aren't more bad guys than we can handle."

"Yes," Matthieu said, his voice much less cheerful than Lu's. "And, there is very little leverage we have. Perhaps when you analyze the data Jean-Luc gave you, we will find something. But I think we want to see if we can get information this time."

"So, the plan is to try and get him to give us information?" I was trying to create a list of questions in my mind. Questions that might make Marran say something he didn't want to. I figured if I could go against an Asian gang, a French smuggler wouldn't be too much of a problem.

"Yes. I will try to set him off guard. Here we are. We will park and walk up the hill." He pulled over into a city parking lot. "It is not too far."

We got the folders full of fake papers – the all-purpose disguise – out of the trunk. It was only a few blocks up this hill, but it was steep. Lu and I were panting by the time we stopped outside yet another faded door. This one was originally red. Matthieu raised an eyebrow and I nodded. By the time someone responded to the doorbell, we had control of our breathing.

A woman opened the door. She was in her fifties by the look of the lines on her face. The cotton dress she wore was thin, a housedress I think it's called. "Durand, *qu'est-ce que vous faites ici?*"

"I am here to speak to your husband," Matthieu said in his official voice.

She stabbed a finger toward Lu and me. "Are these English?"

"They are not fluent in French. As a courtesy, perhaps, we can speak English."

She stepped aside and jerked her head back. "I don't know if he is feeling courteous."

We followed Matthieu into a living room where two men were sitting bent over something on the coffee table. The older man, dressed in an undershirt and blue work pants, looked up as we entered. "*Quoi?*" he rasped.

The woman brought up the rear. "They want to speak to you. You need to speak English."

Annoyance flashed across his face. I could see he wasn't in the habit of putting himself out for anyone. "What do you want, Durand?"

"We have a few questions about a missing woman," Matthieu said.

"That Canadian woman? I already told you I don't know anything about her. Who are these women?"

I did my best cold and impersonal stare back. Matthieu answered him, "They are colleagues."

"I don't like this," Marran said, but then he sent the other man out of the room before adding, "Solange, we will have tea."

When the four of us were alone, he looked Lu and me up and down. "*Non, je n'aime pas ca.* I want her to go." He pointed to Lu.

There was silence for a few seconds, and then Matthieu nodded, and I knew he was going to take the chance to keep her safe and away from Marran. "It would be best to meet at the car."

I saw anger flit across Lu's face before she turned to leave. As she started toward the front door, Marran said, "No, go out the back. I don't want my neighbors gossiping about who is coming and going."

Matthieu looked as though he was going to object, but Lu just turned toward the back door.

I stepped closer and let Matthieu take the lead again.

"We have been given information that a car similar to yours was seen in the neighborhood twice on the evening before Madame Wylie disappeared."

It wasn't something I thought would piss off Marran enough to make a mistake, but it was a good opening salvo.

"So?" Marran took a cup of tea from his wife, who then offered cups to us. "I am not the only one with a car like that."

"No, but you do have a car that fits the description." Matthieu was cold and professional again.

I flipped open my folder and pretended to check something on the papers inside. Marran flicked a look in my direction over the rim of his teacup. "What night was this?"

Matthieu gave him the date.

"One minute." He rose and left us.

Matthieu leaned toward me and whispered, "Take care. I do not like this. I hope he was simply making a point by sending Lu away, but I don't wish to poke the bear."

Marran walked back into the room with a date book in his hands. "I was at a meeting that night, in Marseilles. I couldn't have been in this woman's neighborhood."

"Can you give me the names of others at the meeting?" Matthieu prepared to make notes.

"*Oui*, but my associates would not appreciate having their

business shared with strangers. Durand, we know you, but this woman could be anyone. She leaves before I tell you more."

Matthieu was right. This guy was very much into making points. I wasn't in a position to argue. If he wanted me gone, I'd go. Maybe Matthieu would get something we could use. "I suppose you want me to leave by the back door as well," I said, trying to load a level of disdain into my voice, but Marran just nodded and waited. "I will wait at the car, Lieutenant," I said as I left.

SIXTEEN

When I got to the corner where we'd parked the car, Lu wasn't there. I looked around but there were no cafes or open shops around. It was possible she'd gone looking for something to do while she waited. She wasn't the most patient person I knew.

I went over the interview in my mind. I figured Marran was too smart to say something that gave him away, but maybe there was something he didn't say that I should have picked up on. Or, if not that, something I saw. I checked the street again, but still no sign of Lu. I was starting to get worried. Matthieu would be back soon. I hoped Lu got here first; I didn't know how he would react to her absence.

I leaned against the car as I ran through the scene again. The only thing that seemed odd was that Odette had known the case was closed, but Marran didn't seem to. Maybe we should find her and push a bit harder.

I called Lu's cell phone, but there was no answer. We hadn't bothered with voice mail, so I just hung up.

If I assumed Marran did know about the case, then the question was, why didn't he say anything? He could have ended the conversation fast and gone back to what he was doing. But he decided to play games. The only reason I could come up with was to waste our time, and eventually use it to show he had some power over us.

I saw Matthieu coming down the hill. Then I felt the blood rush away from my brain as I realized that one reason for Marran to waste time was to do something to Lu. And she wasn't back yet. I stepped toward Matthieu. He must have noticed she was missing at the same time I realized she probably wasn't just shopping. He sped up. I ran toward him.

"Where is she?" he asked.

I shook my head. "She wasn't there when I came. I thought maybe she'd gone for a walk. But..."

"Yes, Marran was trying to delay me leaving. He had no information. Well, a few names, but they are not on our list of suspected criminals." He looked around, but Lu didn't materialize.

I started to plan our next steps before panic took complete hold. "I don't think we should split up. I wasn't really paying attention to the surroundings when we got here, so you might end up looking for both of us. Is there some place she could shop? Or something she could be looking at?"

"Yes, we should be together." He took my elbow and we started down the hill. "There are a few stores down here. But do you think she would have wandered off?"

I didn't, but I didn't want to worry him more than necessary. Would it make a difference? Would he go charging back to Marran's and demand to know what he'd done? "I don't know. It was a bit complicated to get back here, but Mrs. Marran told me how to negotiate the first couple of turns, and after that I just walked downhill."

Matthieu stopped walking and looked over his shoulder

toward Marran's house. "I forget that you don't know the town as I do." His normally tanned face had paled to a dull grey and his voice was tight.

"Matthieu, we'll find her. We'll look and if we don't see her soon, you'll call your friends at work and they will help." I gave his arm a reassuring squeeze. "And when we do, I'm telling you now, if you break her heart, I'll break you."

He relaxed slightly under my grip. "I am more worried about my heart than hers. I do not plan to hurt her, but she will be the death of me if she goes missing. Let's go back up the route you took and see if we can get any clues."

I followed him. The route looked much easier on the way up, but it was a warren of little streets that I would call alleys, except alleys didn't usually come with names. At the first intersection, Matthieu left me standing on the sidewalk while he rushed through the maze of streets to the left. When he returned, we carried on up the hill.

At the last turn before Marran's house I called Lu again while I waited for Matthieu to return. Still no answer. My optimism was dwindling fast. Matthieu returned and we looked up the remainder of the hill.

"She is perhaps still in the house. I could go in and ask Madame Marran what she said to Lu."

I wasn't sure we should take the chance of giving Marran any reason to be angry with us. Even if he didn't have Lu, he probably knew something about Audrey. Before I could say so, Matthieu continued, "If we assume the opposite of the worse, then it is possible she turned the wrong way. Does she have a good sense of direction?"

"Yes, but you have a point. What if Marran's wife told her to turn the other way?" I looked at the street with a fresh eye. "You know, if I didn't have directions to take the right fork, I might have gone straight ahead. Both look like they are going downhill."

"It would be like Marran to do something like this to show us he was in control. If Lu went this way, she might not know she was going the wrong way until she arrived at the cemetery." He chewed on his upper lip as he thought. Eventually he said, "We should go back to the car. If she had realized where she went wrong and returned, we would have seen her by now."

"If she could see the harbor, she'd head there," I said, pulling out my cell. "I wish she would answer her phone."

Matthieu took my arm and started down the hill at almost a run. "Call her again when we get to the car."

We made it there in half the time it took us to go up the streets. While Matthieu started the car, I pressed redial on my phone. It connected just as I heard the bell chimes that Lu had picked as her ring tone. It was coming from the region of my feet.

Matthieu looked at me and I said, "Keep going." Then I reached down and scrabbled my fingers under the seat until I found the slim form of Lu's phone.

We drove to the harbor without seeing Lu. Matthieu continued until we reached the cemetery. When he pulled up alongside the entrance, I glanced over the rows of mausoleums, each looking like a model of a house. I thought how Lu would have enjoyed wandering through it and looking at the intricacies of design. But she wouldn't have done that today. She would be doing her best to find us again. "What now? Do we call your friends in the gendarmerie?"

Matthieu shook his head. "I know they will have to wait for her to be gone two days. You know her. If we assume she came this way, what would she have done when she realized she was lost?"

My mind was jumping all over the place. I thought we'd find her at the harbor, but she wasn't there. And she would have made herself visible if she was. "I think we continue to drive. If she got here by taking the wrong turn, there's no guarantee that she would have walked the right way toward the harbor. I can't see a landmark from here. She could have turned left instead."

Matthieu put the car in gear and we headed into the residential area around the cemetery.

WE DROVE around until we were back where we'd parked to visit Marran. Matthieu pulled over to the curb again, and we sat for a few seconds. "What now?" I asked. If it had been Vancouver, I could have figured out what to do. I could have found people to help. Here, I had to rely on Matthieu. I didn't like the feeling of being out of control.

"Stay here. I am going to confront Marran. If he has taken her, I don't want you to become involved in what I will do." He opened his door, and I undid my seatbelt.

"I'm not staying here." I exited the car. "I am not going to let you out of my sight." If Matthieu disappeared like Lu did I had no way to find them and having one missing person was bad enough. I wasn't planning on letting the count go up to three.

He looked at me like he wanted to cuff me to the car. Then he shrugged. "As you wish. If it gets out of hand, I expect you to stay out of the way." All of a sudden, he was the cop not the boyfriend.

We marched up the hill and banged on Marran's door. No one answered. He banged again and still no one came. After a third time, someone shouted from across the street. "*Ils ne sont pas à la maison.*"

I looked toward the sound and saw a man in a wife-beater leaning out of a second story window. Matthieu muttered something under his breath that I didn't catch before shouting back, "*D'accord, quand ont-ils laisser?*"

"*Moins d'une heure.*"

Matthieu waved a hand in thanks and beckoned me to start down the hill again.

"What was that?" I reminded him I couldn't speak French.

"They have left. They must have left while we were searching the streets behind the house. Now we go to hunt down the other places he might be."

When we got back into the car, I started to ask where we would go when a door banged opened up the hill. We both stared in that direction and saw Odette march out of a doorway. She turned and shouted something to whoever was inside. I couldn't understand it, but Matthieu winced.

Odette crossed the street and marched down the other side-walk. Matthieu told me to sit still so she wouldn't notice us. She was muttering as she practically stamped down the hill. I figured he was right, and she wouldn't see us even if we walked smack into her.

"I should have thought about this before," he said. "She knew we were not supposed to be investigating but everyone knows that. The way she said it was different. Do you remember?"

I'd forgotten in the rush to find Lu that I'd had that same thought. "Yes, she said 'wouldn't someone mind if we continued'. Like she knew you'd been ordered to stop."

"So, we are walking again." Matthieu said. "Come, if she doesn't know where Lu is, she will know someone who does."

Odette was so angry with whoever she'd yelled at, that she didn't even look around once. We followed her from a half block away. I hoped Matthieu knew where we were because after the second turn down a twisting street lined with faded doors and shuttered windows, I was completely lost.

"Do you know where she's going?" I asked

"I believe so. It is the back way to the location of the warehouse you told me about."

I started to get my bearings when Odette took a sharp turn to the right when I was expecting her to go straight. We followed her around the corner, and I saw a set of steps facing us. They went up for a block or more. My thighs started to protest at the sight of it.

"MATTHIEU, go ahead if you need to. I'm not sure I'm fit enough to do this." He just waved me on.

We started up the hill together and he didn't pull that far ahead of me. I didn't know how Odette got up there so fast. But then I guess practice numbs the muscles. We stopped at the top and I tried to keep moving my legs so they wouldn't seize up.

Matthieu watched me and then nodded to the gap between buildings. "This passage goes to the street. Your warehouse is another two blocks up. Are you ready?"

I nodded, and we hurried to the street. Odette was just ahead of us, turning into a *Tabac* shop. We walked up the street opposite and watched carefully. The *Tabac* sold newspapers, magazines, cell phone cards, and cigarettes. My guess was Odette was out of cigarettes, so she wasn't going to be long. And no matter how mad she was, she would see us.

"Keep walking up the hill," Matthieu said. "Don't go too far. But maybe she will miss you and concentrate on me."

"What are you going to do?" I wouldn't leave him alone with her unless he had a plan.

"Just speak to her. Don't worry. It will be easier if I can do it in French. I have some secrets of hers that she might want to keep that way. I will talk to her where there are others around."

He clenched his jaw. "If she will not talk to me, I promise I will not do anything to delay our search."

"Okay." I looked him in the eyes and saw control, not the panic that kept sweeping through me. I pointed up the hill. "I'll be in that cafe."

He nodded and waited for me to start walking. I'd taken two steps when my phone rang. I pulled it out of my purse and looked at it. Unknown number. "Hello?"

"Charity, it's me Lu."

I almost passed out with relief. I reached out to stop Matthieu and told him. "Where are you?" I asked Lu.

"I got lost. I've been trying to find you. I'm at Matthieu's cousin's restaurant. I've lost my cell phone. I'm sorry." I could hear the tears in her voice.

"Your phone is in the car. Thank God you are okay. We were thinking the worst. Have a glass of wine and calm down while we get there." I handed the phone to Matthieu.

"*Chérie?* You are okay?" Whatever Lu said, made him smile. "Yes, we will come now. I am glad you are not lost any longer. I promise we will be there before you finish your wine."

As we turned back down hill, I saw Odette walk out of the *Tabac.* She was bent over lighting a cigarette as she left the store, then she looked up, and our eyes met. She said something that was clearly swearing and then spat tobacco off her lip. The woman needed some lessons in etiquette.

I smiled and waved before following Matthieu.

"I think we need to go talk to Odette when we've made sure that Lu is really okay," I said. "She knows something we need, or I'm losing my touch."

Matthieu gestured for me to go ahead of him down the stairs. "I am sure of it, too. There is something she knows."

I turned on the stairs and said, "Maybe we should go talk to her now? Lu is with your cousin and if Odette knows something, we might be able to save Audrey."

Matthieu frowned. I could see he was torn. He really needed to see for himself that Lu was okay. But, the cop in him wanted to pursue the case. "Yes, and if she was going to the warehouse, we might be able to catch her with something we can use to make her talk."

SEVENTEEN

When we got back to the street, Odette was gone. "She can't be that far away. She only just left the store," I said.

"Come," Mathieu said and strode up the hill.

The warehouse was probably our best bet. My feet were going to be killing me tonight, but I didn't need them to dig through the data, so a bowl of ice water to cool the swelling, and a plate of snacks to go with some wine, and I'd be good.

"Maybe you should let me do the talking this time?" I was getting tired of playing the silent foreign authority. "The look she gave me was poisonous. Maybe I can push her into saying something. Maybe I can irritate her into making a mistake." That approach had worked for me more times than I liked to admit. I was becoming reliant on it, which might be a bad thing. I needed more than one way to get information.

He nodded. "You can annoy her as much as you want. She has a temper as you saw. If you can push her hard enough, maybe we'll learn something. But be careful. She is also violent. I will be close, but I have no gun."

I'd been counting on him to back me up. If he wasn't armed, that would be a problem. "No gun? But you're cop."

"I am a gendarme on leave. I have no official use for a gun. Be careful." He glared at me in mock anger. At least I hope it was mock.

I started refining my plan in my head. No need to push too hard. I needed her pissed off enough to make a mistake, but not enough to go postal on us. "Okay I have some experience with violent criminals. Remind me to tell you about the people traffickers I caught last year."

We were once again standing outside the weather-beaten door of the warehouse. It still looked like it hadn't been opened for years. If Odette had just gone in, I thought we would see some evidence.

"We should try the receiving gate," I said, pointing up the hill.

Matthieu shook his head. "This is the door. The receiving gate is only for trucks."

I didn't argue. It was his town, and he would know if a door was right or not. "Okay."

He made a fist and pounded on the door with the edge of it. The sound echoed. He knocked again and then put his ear to the door. "I hear nothing." He stepped back and looked up at the windows on the second floor. They were shuttered, making the whole building look abandoned.

He banged again, but there was no reaction.

"I don't think she's there," I stated the obvious. "Let's go. We can find her again. There's no point in annoying the neighbors. We don't want to announce that we've found their storage site."

He listened at the door again then turned away. Taking my arm to lead me back to the car he said, "Yes. Let us go see how Lu is faring after her adventure. I think we need something to eat after all this exercise."

I hoped that there was an easier route to the car. I guess

there was if you counted walking down steps as being easier than up.

EIGHTEEN

When we got to the restaurant, Lu jumped up and pulled Matthieu into a tight hug. At the sight of them, all of the worry I'd been chewing on for the last hour and a half floated away.

"Do not ever forget your phone again," I said as she let him go and hugged me. "We're having enough trouble finding one missing person."

Matthieu's cousin Pierre brought a plate of appetizers and a chilled bottle of *rosé*. My stomach growled. All those calories I'd burned off on the stairs and hills demanded to be replaced.

Matthieu caught Lu up to date on Odette, and we mulled that over for a while. When the food was all gone, and we came to a lull in our discussion, I noticed Lu and Matthieu were holding hands across the table. I know we needed to find Audrey, but I wanted them to have a bit of time to enjoy each other.

"So, what do we do next?" Lu asked. "It seems there are a lot of connections between Audrey and Odette and that Marran character. We just need to make the connections work, right?"

"Yes." I knew in my gut we had all the pieces we needed to find Audrey. "Does Odette have a fishing boat?"

"No, but that doesn't mean she isn't in control of one through some other means." Matthieu pulled out his notebook and flipped through. "I don't seem to have anything here that would indicate who she might control." He let out a sigh.

The notebook couldn't possibly hold enough information to solve this case, or even a simple crossword puzzle. "Don't you have computerized records?"

"Yes, and my colleagues are constantly reminding me that we have arrived in the twenty-first century. But I believe that some of the newer gendarmes are too interested in using the computer, and not enough interested in doing real investigation. I suppose that makes me sound old."

"Not at all," Lu said. "The computer is just a tool."

I smiled. "You know it's the best tool in the box, though. I couldn't do my job without it."

"I remain to be convinced of that," Matthieu said. "Perhaps this case will help me make a few steps toward the new era of technology?"

I laughed. Maybe he solved his cases through charm. "Is there a database of boat owners outside of the station?" I asked.

"No," Matthieu said before finishing his wine. "I can probably go back and get more information. What are you thinking we need?"

"If you can find out which boats are potentially under Odette's control, it will help Charity with the harbor traffic data." Lu patted his arm. "Can you get access?"

"Yes, but we must be circumspect. If I am seen looking through the database, my reputation as a Luddite might be in danger." He laughed and called for the bill.

His cousin shook his head and pointed at Lu, "It is already paid, Matthieu."

"Thank you," he said. "It is not necessary for you to do that."

"It's not a problem," Lu said.

If they were serious, she was going to have to let him know that she was loaded. If he had a problem with it, they'd have to hash it out.

WE ARRIVED at the office to hear that the Colonel was away. Matthieu grinned and said, "That makes it easier. Come, we can use my office. We must be careful. It is unusual for me to bring civilians into the station." He led us back to his office and we settled in the chairs while he pulled a laptop out of a drawer along with a handful of cables.

I tried not to laugh as he set it up. He seemed to know what he was doing, but he had definitely proven the Luddite label by the way he carefully checked everything he plugged in.

He typed in his password and settled back while the laptop booted. "Now, it will take a moment for me to get access to the data, but her records will show known associates. I should know who of them own boats."

"If you can get printouts, we will be able to check against the harbor data." I was worried that someone would come in and demand to know why he was accessing data when he was supposed to be away. But Matthieu seemed relaxed, and I had to take my cue from him.

He noticed me glance at the door and started typing. "Yes, it would be best to spend as little time as possible here. I don't know who else saw us come in. Dominique would not tell anyone I am here, but if one of the Colonel's flunkies saw us, we'll be asked to leave."

"What exactly is going on here, Matthieu?" Lu asked. "It looks to me like you are five minutes away from being fired every day."

"It is not that bad, but you are right, I am not all that popular with the new regime. And, if I am honest, I have not made an effort to be so," he said tapping keys with his two index fingers. "Ah, here we are. Okay, it will be on the printer as we leave."

He shut down the laptop.

At least he was competent when he used a computer. All it would take is a bit of an adjustment in his attitude and he'd be right in this century. "Do you really hate the computer, or is it something you do to annoy the boss?" I asked.

He put the laptop back in the drawer and grinned. "A little of both, I think. If we used it appropriately, I would have no problem with this." He tapped the back-plastic casing. "But it is not meant to be the only tool. So, it started as a little rebellion, and now I am, how do you say, trapped in the lie."

Matthieu asked us to wait outside the door to the printer room. "It would not be good to have someone declare information was compromised by your presence."

FIFTEEN MINUTES later we were settled in the dining room. I really wanted to start knocking on doors in Marran's neighborhood. Audrey had been missing too long for me to feel comfortable sitting here with a computer. I had to remind myself that investigation was about more than kicking in doors and interrogating bad guys. My more rational side knew spending time analyzing the data would probably be the best thing. If it didn't lead us to Audrey, it would at least tell us what door to kick in.

As I waited for the security settings to run, I said, "I don't want to just try to prove Odette has control over a boat that has some schedule link to Marran. My original idea was to use time as a filter for the data we got from Jean-Luc. We might find boats that had a connection to each other."

"How long do you think this will take?" Matthieu asked. "It

is late now and if we are going to follow up on any leads, we might have to go into some unsavory places."

"Are you thinking you don't want us joining you?" Lu's voice took on an edge I didn't usually hear. Matthieu needed to tread very carefully here. I looked up, hoping to see him realize his mistake.

He pursed his lips before shaking his head and saying, "I was thinking that we need to be prepared."

Smart answer.

"It's going to take a couple of hours at least," I said, typing in the URL. "We'll need to test our assumptions as we find linkages between the different data points."

"I'll make some phone calls then," he said, standing to take out his phone. "If we need to find Marran or Odette, I'll find out where they are likely to be. But you know, if we take too long to make the connections, we will not go out until morning, and Marran will be out on his boat again."

"How long is too long?" I was typing in a search parameter while I waited. I hoped for a result that looped each boat in and out of the harbor. Marran's boats would still be colored, but I could highlight other boats as needed.

"If we don't start out in the next three hours, we will have to wait until tomorrow afternoon for Marran. Odette is a different matter. She will be at home in the morning to take care of her mother again."

He started talking into the phone, so Lu and I concentrated on the data. We removed some of the boats that were clearly not intersecting with any of those Marran controlled.

"These three." Lu pointed to dots that seemed to either follow or lead Marran's.

"Good catch." I removed all boats except the ones we wanted. "Look, they all intersect with Marran's path on the way in."

"Can you show how long each boat is out?" Lu asked. And when I plotted the six of them, she added, "No, all of them. I'm thinking if these boats all take longer than average, maybe Marran picks up the contraband and transfers it. Remember the church? Smugglers need secrecy, which means complications."

"Good point." I ran the query with all six boats identified in red. "Yes, look, all of them come in above average times."

I wrote down the names of the boats and looked up the owners. Matthieu was still talking on the phone. "We need to do some testing. Lu, write down a list of queries that we can test. Things like query boats that run consistently under or over average, boats that skip days, you know."

Lu picked up a pencil and started making notes. She looked up to ask, "Should you test this over different periods? That data covers the last two weeks, right?"

"Yeah, great idea. And maybe all this will help Matthieu with his career. I'm not sure finding Audrey and actually closing the already closed case will do the trick. But catching a smuggling ring should get him some brownie points." I started running queries while we waited for him to get off the phone.

Ten minutes later, he clicked his cell shut and joined us. I had made notes about what we'd found, all the while cursing the lack of printer.

"Well?" he asked. "Have you found something? Am I about to be converted to the side of the computers?"

"We have five boats that have a connection. Look." I displayed the reports we'd run. "We think Marran is offloading the stuff to other boats because they aren't likely to be searched. That way every time his boats are searched, they're clean."

"Do you have names of the boats?" he asked. I handed him the list with the owners' names. "Hmm, well. I see we have something to speak to Arnaud Marran about. Also, here is the name of the Colonel's brother. Interesting, no?"

"Is that a surprise?" Lu asked.

"Yes and no." He looked at his watch. "We can talk to Marran at his favorite bar. My contact says he is settled in for the night."

I let the cryptic comment go for now. "Is confronting him in public a good idea?"

"We will not confront. I think we can drop a few choice words in his ear and perhaps persuade him to come to a more private place. If not, we will leave, and keep him under observation."

"Give us a couple of minutes," Lu said. "If we are going to be doing surveillance at night, darker clothes might be better."

I WAS RELIEVED to find that the bar was not at the top of a steep hill that was too narrow for cars. My legs would get a break. It was along a narrow side street directly off the harbor. The interior was dark, but each table had a candle. I couldn't see any women inside, not even a waitress. The bartender was busy pouring an amber liquid into tiny glasses. There was a cloud of smoke floating to the ceiling, despite the laws against smoking in bars and restaurants.

"Matthieu, it might be better if we stayed outside," I said. "I think we might attract the wrong kind of attention."

"Yes, that is true." At least he tried to disguise the relief in his voice. "If you go along to the *Orange* store, you can pretend to look at the latest in cell phone technology. You'll also be able to see the bar reflected in the window."

"Very well-organized street," I said.

"Be careful," Lu said, giving him a peck on the cheek. Then we left him and strolled along the street as though we hadn't a care in the world.

Standing outside the phone store, we kept our eyes on the reflection. Matthieu walked up to the bar and ordered a drink.

I turned to look at Lu and saw her feelings painted across her face. "You know, Lu, he's a very smart man. You need to be careful there."

A giant grin crossed her face. "You noticed that, huh? If he had told us we couldn't come in, we would have argued. I like that he trusted us to be sensible."

I nodded. "Have you talked about what you are going to do?"

"It's only been a couple of days, Charity. I don't want to scare him off."

I didn't think she could scare him off no matter what she did. "Why don't you invite him to come to Paris? It could be a trial run for your relationship."

We watched as Matthieu wandered over to Marran. He sat down and started talking. To the casual observer, they would look like friends. A casual observer wouldn't see the tension in Matthieu's posture or the menace in the way Marran lounged in his chair.

"I was thinking of it," Lu confessed. "I would like to see him outside a criminal investigation, and on neutral ground. I want Jake to meet him, too."

"Get the guy's perspective?"

Matthieu stood up and put his glass on the bar on his way out. No one followed him, but Marran was laughing, and I don't think it was at a joke.

"Yes. I trust Jake's opinion. In his business, he meets a lot of people who are not what they seem."

Matthieu joined us at the window. "He is unnerved."

"He's making a call." I nodded to the reflection in the store window. "Should we move on?"

Matthieu took my elbow and said, "Wait. I want to see his reaction. Then we will go."

Marran talked rapidly into the phone, then put it back in his pocket. "He's rattled all right. That was all business."

"We should go to the car. I—" his phone played the opening notes of Aretha Franklin's RESPECT. "One moment."

I looked at the reflection again and noticed Marran watching. I pulled Lu away from the window into the shadows as Matthieu started speaking in French. I didn't understand the words, but he sounded like he was arguing with someone.

Marran was still watching. I was pretty sure his call wasn't to get someone to hide evidence. He was making a power play.

Matthieu was still arguing on the phone.

"This isn't good, Lu." I nodded to the bar window.

Matthieu snapped his phone shut. "Ladies, we must leave now."

"What just happened?" Lu asked.

He started toward the car. "When we are somewhere else. I am currently a little too angry to tell you what I think."

Lu held out her hand for the car keys. "I'll drive. And we are going home, where you will tell us what we need to know."

NINETEEN

When we pulled up to the house, Lu parked Matthieu's car behind ours in the driveway. He'd seemed to calm down a little on the short drive, and I saw her hand him back the keys as I followed them along the path. I glanced around, fearing to see a thug lurking in the shadows of the garden, but all I saw was a quick twitch of the curtains in Claudette's window. She was going to have a lot to gossip about. I just hoped our comings and goings were all we would give her tonight.

We settled in the living room before Lu said, "Okay, Matthieu, talk."

Matthieu paused, took off his jacket, and then placed his phone on the table. He fussed with the cushion, and I was about to tell him to get on with it, when he said, "The call was from the Colonel. I have been ordered to leave Arnaud Marran alone. I am not to go near him, or his home, or his wife, on penalty of my job, and possibly my freedom."

Now I understood his anger. "You think Marran called him?"

Matthieu nodded and drew his hands through his hair. "Yes, and I am told that if I do anything to annoy this upstanding member of our community, I will be immediately suspended and possibly charged with harassment."

Lu put coffee on the table before sitting next to Matthieu on the couch. "I know it's late, but I don't think we are going to be getting any sleep tonight anyway, so we might as well enjoy the coffee." She turned to Matthieu and said, "You didn't seem surprised to get the call."

"I was. But now that I think of it, I should have known something like that would happen. Everything we are finding out is giving me confirmation of what I am suspecting for a while now. I think my colonel is, how do you say? Bent?"

I didn't know what to say. Matthieu didn't seem all that upset, but it must have meant something to him that the man who has been making his work life miserable was a crook. It was clear he loved the job. Well, maybe not the job, but the investigation. It wasn't just Lu that had drawn him to work with us; it was his love for puzzles.

"So, do you report him to someone? Will he be removed?" I asked.

He stirred sugar into his cup before answering. "No, it would be nice to have someone who would put in the effort to clean up the corruption, but no one will be interested in removing the Colonel. He is not causing enough trouble. We will need to work carefully now. But given what we found in the boat route analysis, we may be able to hurt the colonel's family. And we can do that within the rules I have just been given."

"Matthieu," Lu said. "I don't want you to lose your job. Maybe you can tell us what we can do. You don't need to come with us."

He took her hand and kissed the back of it. "I will not let you go into danger without me by your side. You and Charity are brave and capable, but these people are exceedingly dangerous."

"But you have a life here that might be destroyed if you continue." Lu took her hand back. "I don't want you to regret helping us."

"There are many things I will regret in my life but helping you to find Madame Wylie will not be one of them."

"And your job? Your reputation?" I needed to know that he wouldn't suddenly go all cop on us.

"Charity, that job has been getting impossible for a very long time. I think, perhaps, I have been afraid to leave, or perhaps too... I don't know, not angry... I think apathetic is more correct. If I lose my rank or even the job, then so be it." He turned to Lu and reached for her hand. "My reputation is strong enough to withstand whatever comes. If not, then it isn't worth worrying about."

The heat in his voice told me he was serious. This wasn't just a bit of flattery to get Lu into bed. If he was willing to throw away everything he had here, I had an idea. "If you are prepared to use a computer as the tool it is, you might make a good PI."

He laughed and said, "You know, perhaps you are right. But that is a discussion for later. You may do your best to convert, or educate me, when we have Madame Wylie safely at home."

There didn't seem to be much more to say. We returned to the data on the boats. Matthieu looked at the ones we'd found that intersected with Marran's. "It is possible the captain is not the one involved. Let me think of who might have been on the boats. If the captain is not on board, the crew will have the power to do what they will. If we don't find a culprit, perhaps we will find someone who will answer questions."

As he started writing a list of names, I looked at the data labels. "Matthieu, what is the French word for crew?"

"*L'équipage*. Why? Are you suggesting you can find this information from the database?"

"Yes, the data is here, give me a minute." I ran the query.

"See," I said, pointing to the list of names. "I guess it's possible that these people were just the names they gave, and others were on the boat."

He looked at the list. "These three men were Odette's lovers at one time or another. This one is also Marran's godson, I had forgotten that relationship. I think we have our link between Odette and Marran."

"Will she be home? Can we go now?" Lu started clearing the coffee cups away.

"It is too late to go knocking on her door without risking her neighbors calling the police," Matthieu said.

"No. Audrey has been missing for too long," I said. "We should go now."

Matthieu looked at Lu, whether for support or for an indication how to handle me, I didn't know. "I do not think the Colonel is going to ignore our investigation if we continue to annoy Marran. It will not help if we are thrown in the jail until he can find a way to control us."

I opened my mouth to argue, but realized he was right before I got any words out. I took a breath and said, "You're right. As much as I want to find Audrey fast, the last thing we need is another call from the crooked colonel telling us to stay away from Odette Pilon." I didn't know about Lu and Matthieu, but I definitely needed respite from all the coffee we'd been drinking. I was starting to get the caffeine trembles. When that happens, I usually don't make good decisions.

"If we go early in the morning, we can catch her before she is truly awake," Matthieu said. "She will possibly be easier to manipulate if we talk to her before her morning espresso."

I figured it was time for me to retire so they could pretend I didn't know he would stay overnight. "Sounds like a plan. I'm done. See you at six." I told myself I would get to sleep no matter how much caffeine was coursing through my veins.

TWENTY

Five hours later, I came down to the kitchen and found Lu waiting for me.

She pulled a croissant out of the oven and said, "We've got time for breakfast. Grab a coffee and come into the dining room."

I did as I was told and found Matthieu sitting at the table when I followed Lu there. "So how are we going to do this? Good cop, bad cop, other cop?" I asked as I smeared butter on the croissant.

Matthieu laughed. "I think you have a good idea. But she seems to dislike all of us, so I am not sure there is an opportunity to be good cop."

I remembered the look she gave me last night from the *Tabac*. "She thinks she has something on us. She's feeling a little cocky, can we attack that? We can hint that we know. We can—"

"I could out sneer her," Lu said. "The Asian ice princess is always useful in ego battles. And she might not have run into it before."

Matthieu pursed his lips in thought before speaking. "I do

not know what she thinks she has on us, but we do have knowledge that she doesn't know we have. If you are willing to allow me to make a suggestion, I think we should attempt this approach. You and Lu will do the speaking this time. I will be the silent menace. If she will not speak to you in English, I will act as the interpreter and provoke her to English by paraphrasing her words so that she has to clarify."

"Okay, let's go shake up Odette," I said, swallowing the last of the coffee, and topping up the jitters. I promised myself I'd drink enough water to flush out the caffeine when I had time.

We piled into the car and headed to the house on the hill. Matthieu drove while Lu and I worked out the details of the plan.

I would take the lead using my skill as a PI, and she would be the one to carry the arrogance bag. I hoped Matthieu could stand the performance. Lu could be one mean bitch when she put her mind to it.

AFTER HE PARKED THE CAR, we marched up the hill portraying our officiousness for the neighbors if they were watching.

Matthieu banged on the door without announcing himself until Odette yanked it open shouting, "*Arrêter de faire tant de bruit!* Oh, Durand and his little harem. What is so urgent that you batter my door?"

I stepped forward and said, "We have some questions for you." I didn't wait for her to invite me in, I just kept moving forcing her to step aside to allow me past. I heard Lu and Matthieu follow and a quiet hiss of French from Odette. No idea what the words were, but the translation was probably something like 'why the fuck am I standing here holding the door for these assholes?'

If it had been me, I would have just gone out and closed the door behind me. But then maybe Odette had something in here to protect from our prying eyes. Whatever the reason, I liked the way the interview started. Now we needed to take advantage of the upper hand.

We reached the kitchen and I gestured for Odette to sit, wondering how long she'd cede control.

"You are aware we are looking for Audrey Wylie?" I didn't wait for her to answer. "We have information that you are involved. We are prepared to negotiate your situation if you tell us where she is."

"You have nothing. This investigation is closed." She started to stand, and Lu held up a hand to halt her.

Odette opened her mouth to protest, but Lu raised an eyebrow just a little bit and said, "This investigation is no longer in the hands of the local authorities. I'm sure you know that this is far more than an investigation into a missing woman."

"You won't get anywhere with your stupid questions," Odette snapped. "You have no power to do anything in this town." This time she stood, walked to the stove, and started to make coffee.

Lu continued in a voice that dropped the temperature in the room by five degrees, "I am sure your petty politics here are difficult for the locals to deal with. But Mrs. Wylie is a Canadian citizen and as such deserves the protection of our authorities." It sounded good to me.

Odette turned from the stove and sneered back at Lu. "That woman was putting her nose into things that didn't concern her. If she is missing, it is her own fault for not heeding advice."

"Is that why you were at her house? To give her advice?" Lu asked, looking down at Odette who was at least three inches shorter.

"I am not a counselor." Odette turned back to the stove and

kept her eyes on the pot. I knew we were losing the power position, but she still wasn't sure who we were and what leverage we had. I could see the calculations going on behind her narrowed eyes and thinned lips.

It was time for me to join the conversation. "If she has come to harm, and you were known to have helped us, there may be a way for you to escape punishment. Otherwise, your mother may have to find someone else to take care of her."

She spun away from the stove, and I was taken aback by the fury in her eyes. "My mother is in a hospice now. You let her die in peace." She grabbed a cigarette from a pack on the counter. "It does not matter anyway. Punishment comes from places you do not control. I will not provide you with any information. I do not care what the authorities offer, no matter where those authorities come from."

I smiled. "So, you do have information."

"No. And do not try to trick me. I have friends who will protect me from anything you can do." She flicked her fingers in dismissal and turned back to the now ready coffee. Taking down a single cup she filled it and added sugar.

Lu inspected her nails as she said, "Yes, we are dealing with that now. I think you may find your friends are too busy with their own problems to protect you. If you are of no use to us, then perhaps we should simply leave you to their displeasure."

This time it was Odette's turn to smile. "So. You are aware of the Colonel's little vice. Well, that doesn't change anything. I will not tell you what you want to know."

I don't know why she went from angry and scared to calm and back in control, but I knew that we had lost our opportunity to win this confrontation. "We know about that and we know about what Arnaud Marran is doing as well."

She sipped her coffee before answering, "I advise you to leave that particular situation alone."

I smiled. "If you think Marran will protect you, you are being naive. Someone with your background can't afford to be naive, can they? If he needs to throw you to the sharks, he won't hesitate."

She slapped the coffee cup on the counter and turned to me. The fury in her eyes was reinforced by the blaze of color across her cheeks. "Get out. Get out of my house."

I nodded for Lu and Matthieu to leave. Before I joined them in the hall, I gave Odette a look from top to bottom, and then shook my head. "A pity. So much potential wasted."

She opened a drawer that was filled with knives, and I hurried to follow Matthieu and Lu to the street.

TWENTY-ONE

On the street, I took a deep breath. "What the hell did I say to set her off?"

Matthieu shook his head and led us to the cafe down the street. When we had coffee and a second round of breakfast pastry in front of us, he answered me, "I think you just shook her up. No matter how much she pretends, it must be hard for her to realize her mother is about to die. I would like to know what the little vice is of our esteemed colonel. It might be useful for the future." His smile faded. "Ah, but she is right, nothing will change."

Lu shrugged. "Matthieu, what do you care? You are going to quit, aren't you?"

"Yes. I haven't changed my mind, don't worry." He kissed her cheek. "But I was thinking of some of my friends who might need to have a little leverage to allow them to be more effective. But that does not explain why she suddenly became confident."

I thought back to the last big case and the surprise we got when we thought we were done. "Is there a chance that someone we don't know about is running this organization? Maybe she realized we didn't know about the big boss?"

Matthieu shook his head. "No. We know there are others in this scheme. Marran is selling the guns to someone after all. And I wouldn't be surprised if the Russians, or some terrorists, are involved. But they are not running the show here. They don't let someone outside their organizations have any power, but they expect their suppliers to take care of their own business. So, they will act against Marran if something goes wrong."

"I think it's Marran," Lu said. "She believes he'll protect her. I think she was surprised that you knew the connection, but you pushed her over the edge with the comments about Marran."

"Ladies, I think it is time for us to leave." Matthieu pointed up to Odette's door. The woman looked directly at us and stormed off up the hill.

"How are we going to follow her?" Lu asked. "It's not like we can hide in the shadows."

Matthieu handed Lu his keys. "She will expect us to follow, but we will use that. You both take the car. I will follow on foot."

"But we don't know where she's headed. How will we—" I stopped talking when Matthieu held up his phone. "Okay. So, she won't know where we are. Get going."

I dropped enough money on the table to more than cover the bill and ran back to the car after Lu.

When we got there, Lu's phone rang. She tossed it to me and unlocked the doors.

I flipped it open. "Matthieu?"

"Yes, I have her in sight. I believe she is going to *Le Bateau,* a bar where all the fishermen meet. It is like their club, where they sort out who works where and when. I think you would call it a union hall. If I am correct, you need to turn toward the harbor. When you reach a corner with a restaurant called *Le Bouffon*, tell me, and then turn right. I will give you more instructions then."

I could hear the street noises around Matthieu as we drove,

but he didn't say more. I wondered if Odette was watching him, leading him on, or into a trap. I kept that thought to myself. Lu needed to be able to concentrate on her driving.

The traffic was getting a bit heavier, and she kept her eyes on the road. Cars seemed to pop out of side streets with no regard to who was on the road. Lu swore at a couple of pedestrians who just stepped out into traffic. Then another car swung into the gap between ours and the one ahead. Lu slammed on the brakes. I jerked against the seatbelt, swearing.

"Relax, I've got this," Lu said, laughing. "You know how well I drive."

Yes, I knew how she drove at home where the roads were wide – like a NASCAR driver. I turned my attention to looking for the restaurant. It was almost as hard as avoiding an accident. There were stores, cafes, and bistros lining both sides of the street.

"There." I pointed a block ahead. "Turn right." I put the phone back to my ear. "Matthieu, we're there."

"Good, drive straight ahead until you can see a fountain in the center of the square. I think about five streets. She is still headed in your direction."

We made our way to the square. The fountain was in the middle of a roundabout. I told Matthieu and he didn't answer. So, I told Lu, "Go around until I get more directions."

We'd circled twice before Matthieu started speaking again. I could see old men on benches laughing at the stupid tourists. "Go to the harbor and park near Jean-Luc's office. Do you know the way?"

Lu nodded when I asked her. "So, she's changed directions?"

"No. Mademoiselle Pilon is far too good at losing a tail."

. . .

WHEN MATTHIEU JOINED us at the harbor, he took over the driver's seat and Lu jumped in the back. "I think we must do something other than try to break one of these damn criminals. I am proposing that we split up. I do not like it, but it has been too many days, and Madame Wylie may not much longer if she is, indeed, still alive. I am sorry to suggest we may be too late. We must concentrate on that part of the case. The gun smuggling will come later."

I agreed with Matthieu, but when he said split up, I hoped he meant Lu would stay with me or him. I wanted her safe. She wasn't an investigator, and, unlike us, she didn't have the skills to deal with what could come up. "Lu should stay with the car."

"I will not just sit here while you go off and rescue Audrey," Lu announced.

I tried another tactic. "Okay, then you have to stay with Matthieu or me. I don't think you should go by yourself."

"Don't you think I can handle myself?" Lu eyes were narrowed, and I knew there was no point in arguing further.

"Okay," I said.

"Lu, do you have any experience in self-defense?" Matthieu asked while I was trying to come up with a plan that kept her safe.

"No." She was calmer. "But that doesn't mean I'll sit on the sidelines."

"Very well. We all have our telephones, yes?" Matthieu asked. "We will keep in touch at all times. If any of us feels in too much danger, they must speak up. We will decide what to do then. If we cannot reach someone when we call, we all return here, yes?"

Lu and I nodded. "Where do we search?" Lu asked, taking her phone back from me.

"I will go to Marran's. He is at sea right now, so maybe I can bully his wife into giving me the information we need. Charity,

I think that you may find Odette around that cemetery. She was going in that direction when I lost her. You are used to keeping yourself safe I think, but there are abandoned houses in that area so be careful. It may be where they are holding Madame Wylie."

I nodded. "Maybe I should concentrate on looking for Audrey and just try to avoid Odette."

"And me?" Lu asked still bristling.

"It is possible that Odette is keeping Madame Wylie near her home. It would be useful to see if you can find our missing redhead. Walk around the streets near the *Le Bateau* keeping your eyes open for her. When we find out where she has been, we can search for any hideouts." He nodded as though checking an item off his list. "I will drive you as close as I can to save on time. Are your phones ready? I do not wish to have a battery run out at the worst time."

We checked, and we all had hours left on the phones. Matthieu took a U-turn and headed toward the cemetery.

"Do we leave our phones on?" Lu asked. "Use them like we just did?"

"No. Not necessary, just place it on vibrate. Be sure to call if you find something." Matthieu pulled over to the side of the cemetery. "Charity, these streets are complicated. Do you think you can keep your direction?"

I pulled the GPS out of my purse. "I can put the cemetery as a favorite location and then home back in on it."

"I am coming to believe that there is something to this technology business." He waited until I was across the road before driving off with Lu.

TWENTY-TWO

I set the location and started with the center of three streets. The sign posted on the wall of the building was *Rue Pastis*. It kept coming up everywhere like a subliminal ad. I figured I was going to have to drink a little of this stuff.

I glanced up the street to see the familiar row of stone walls broken by doorways. Windows were shuttered, and every home looked abandoned. I hoped I would be able to tell the actual abandoned ones from the ones just locked up for the day. There were no cars in sight. No people on the street.

I walked past a few doors, keeping my eyes on both sides of the street. The first few were for inhabited homes. I heard a bird squawking behind one door and could smell the aromas of cooking wafting out of the shutters of the next one. So, the shutters could be closed but the windows open. That helped, I just needed to be close enough to listen, or smell the signs of activity without looking suspicious.

"I hope no one is watching, because it's going to look like I'm casing the joint." I was muttering to myself again, not a good sign.

I worked my way to the first intersection. Across the street was a store. The sign said *Boulangerie* which I knew meant bakery, but the shutters were down, and it looked permanently closed. I looked up and down the street. It seemed to get dirtier to the left, so I went that way. Was it bad that I identified dirty with abandoned?

I heard a vehicle coming. I tried to look casual as the van went by, but I'm pretty sure it didn't work. How was I supposed to be casual on a basically empty street? The van passed without stopping.

The first house I came to on this street was clearly abandoned. The door was festooned in spider webs and the shutters were hanging loosely from the hinges. I tried to suppress the shivers as I used my hand to clear the webs. No spiders were visible, but I still felt something crawling along my arm. Nothing was there when I looked, but I shuddered and brushed at the sensation anyway. The door was locked tight. I decided it made sense to check out a few more of the doors on the street before trying to break into a locked door. Go for the easier ones first.

Before I reached for the next door my purse buzzed. I pulled out the phone and saw it was Lu. "News?" While I waited for her to answer, I pushed at the cracked yellow wood, no spiders, but it was jammed on the frame.

"I found Odette, and I'm following her now." She was barely audible. "I can't get Matthieu on the line. Can you try and call me back?"

I moved to the next house, looking around but still no one was watching me. "I'll try in a minute. It's probably fine but give me a chance to look in on these places. I've one more on this side, and two on the other. If he doesn't answer by then, you head back to the harbor."

The pause before she answered worried me. "Okay. I'll keep calling too. Maybe he's busy questioning Marran's wife."

We hung up and I tested the last house on this side, nothing. I hurried across the street and started making my way back down. A blue door with a big hole worn in the top opened when I pushed. I slipped inside. There was no one around. The stairs had collapsed a long time ago by the depth of the dust on the wreckage. I checked the small yard through the kitchen window. No sign of anything other than brown weeds.

I noticed a ladder on the side wall of the garden. A wall that abutted the next abandoned home. The kitchen door was sealed with a thick crossbar of wood. I wrapped my jacket around my arm and said a silent sorry to whoever actually owned the house before smashing the glass in the window.

I managed not to cut myself as I pulled out the shards and climbed through. I tested the ladder and decided it would hold, so I scrambled up and dropped down into the yard next door.

This one was in a bit better shape. The ground was covered in terracotta tiles, there were pots around the edge filled with dead plants, but it was tidy at least. I tested the door, but it didn't budge. I swore quietly and checked the window. It was cracked, but I was going to have to break another sheet of glass.

This time, climbing in, I nicked my leg on the glass. Just a shallow cut, but I had to stop to stem the blood. I didn't have anything to wrap it, but a bit of pressure was enough. I'd just have to be careful until I could find some bandages.

I made my way into the hall and noticed that the stairs were still intact. A glance in the front room showed no disturbance in the dust. I walked back to the kitchen to check for a basement, but there were no doors other than the one to the yard. Back at the stairs, I checked out the treads. I wasn't happy about the idea of going up to find myself trapped if they collapsed. They looked firm, so I put my purse on the first stair just in case I was going to have to fight my way out, and I ran up.

There were two rooms with a bathroom in between. The

bathroom was clean and looked like it had been recently scoured. I felt a leap of hope. The first door opened on what had been a craft room, a sewing machine, and some turned over baskets of knitting supplies. All covered in a film of dust. The second door was locked.

"Audrey?" I called through it, but no one answered. I threw myself against the door. The only result was a sore shoulder and a seeping of blood from the cut on my leg.

I looked around for something that would help me through. The door was solid, and I couldn't expect to ram it open, because the hall wasn't wide enough to build up any force. I'd have to find a different way to get it open. There were no hinges, so I couldn't try removing them and pop the lock, but the keyhole looked like I could jimmy it. Picking locks was definitely a skill for a private investigator.

I went back down to get my purse. Inside was a plastic rattail comb that might work, and I found my Leatherman tool. A flash of red plastic reminded me I was supposed to call Matthieu. I tried his number, but it rang onto voicemail. I called Lu, but her phone rang busy. I couldn't risk having my phone buzz while I was breaking into the locked room, so I turned it off. Promising myself I would turn it back on in a couple of minutes.

Back upstairs, I pulled the Leatherman out and flipped it to open the tools. Like a Swiss Army knife, it contained a couple of screwdrivers and a pair of pliers. Unfortunately, they were all too short to jimmy the lock.

I took the comb out and used the tail to wiggle the tumblers of the lock. It didn't work. The plastic was too thick to get far enough into the hole.

I put my ear to the door. I thought I heard something banging in there. I stepped back, literally, and mentally. "What else can you use? Think."

I went back to the other room. A knitting needle, or thin crochet hook, would be perfect. The baskets were filled with half completed projects. Yarn and knitting needles in one, cotton and crochet hooks in another. I thanked whoever arranged the universe that the prior owner had liked to make lace. There were two fine hooks that would be perfect. I grabbed them and a cloud of dust made me sneeze.

Back at the door, I slid one hook in the hole and used the other to manipulate the pins inside. A couple of clicks and the door was unlocked. I pushed it open, and there in the middle of the room, was a woman gagged and tied to a chair.

"Audrey?"

She struggled to nod. I removed the gag and untied her.

"Hurry, she'll be back soon," Audrey gasped.

"Can you walk?" I was surprised at how healthy she looked. "Are you okay?"

"They feed me, and I get some exercise. I'll be fine when I get out of here," she said then looked at my leg. "Never mind me, you're bleeding."

I looked at my leg and realized the blood seep was getting worse. "I'm fine. I'll get it fixed later; it won't get any worse at least. Are you sure you are okay?"

"I am capable of getting out of here. I've been in worse situations and survived." She rolled her shoulders and winced. "I'll be sore for a couple of days, I'm sure."

Despite her words, Audrey groaned when she stood. We made our way downstairs and got out the front door without a problem. I turned my phone on as we crossed the street. It buzzed immediately. "Lu, I've got Audrey."

"Thank goodness. Have you heard from Matthieu?"

Shit! "No. How long has it been?"

"It feels like a half hour, but I think it's been about ten

minutes since I first tried to call him. Charity, what if they have him?"

I looked at Audrey and saw she was looking healthy enough to hurry. I turned back to the phone. "How far from the cemetery are you?"

"A few blocks away. Odette is ahead of me; she's turning up one of the streets where we left you." Her voice was full of tension.

"We have to go," I said to Audrey. "Odette Pilon is on her way, and we don't want to be in sight when she gets here." I put the phone back to my face and said, "We'll go uphill. I'm sure it will lead back somewhere I recognize. Keep trying Matthieu. As soon as Audrey is safe, I'll call you back and we can go find him."

Audrey and I headed up the street and turned right when we got to the top. My leg was burning with the effort, but Audrey strode purposefully along. "If we continue to go this way, we will arrive at a clinic where a friend of mine works," Audrey said. "I will be safe, your leg will be tended to, and then you can get on with whatever your friend on the phone needs."

"Thank you," I said. I didn't want to leave her, but if she said she felt safe, I'd trust her.

We turned a corner and I saw the green neon cross that indicated a pharmacy.

Audrey hurried at the sight of it. She looked at me as I hobbled beside her. "Now, tell me who you are, and why you are here?"

I told her about Delores' request and how Matthieu and Lu were also trying to rescue her.

"I see. Well, Matthieu Durand is a good man. I suppose you have learned about the guns."

We reached the clinic a minute later. It was full when we arrived, but it seemed Audrey did have friends inside because I was whisked into the back room, cleaned up, stitched, and sent on my way within ten minutes.

"I have to go help Lu," I said. "Are you sure you can stay here for a while? Then we can get you back to the house. Um, we've been staying there."

She patted my hand and said, "No problem. You take care of your friend and we'll talk later."

TWENTY-THREE

I left Audrey and headed toward the cemetery, pulling out my cell phone as I walked. "Lu, any news?"

"No. And now I've lost Odette." There was a shake to her voice I didn't like to hear.

"Are you at the cemetery?" I was glad when she said she was. It was only a couple of turns to get me back to her. "I'll be there in a few minutes."

"Do you remember how to get to Marran's house?" she asked, panic straining her voice.

I sped up. My leg didn't like that, so I was doing a fast limp, more like a hop than a walk. "No, but I have the GPS. It will find the fastest way there."

I rounded the corner and saw her standing with the phone to her ear looking into the rows of mausoleums. Perhaps meeting at a cemetery wasn't the smartest thing to do. "Call him again," I said then clicked the phone shut.

I dropped it in my purse and brought out the GPS. I pressed the button to turn it on and watched it run through the starter screens as I crossed the road to stand beside her.

Lu took the phone from her ear and shook her head. "He's still not answering."

I gave her a hug and felt her trembling in my arms. When I pulled back, I said, "We'll find him, don't worry. We found Audrey. We'll find Matthieu."

I saw tears in her eyes, but then she blinked them away before saying, "Do you have the address we need?"

I held up the GPS. "Nope. But it goes to points of interest too. I figure a church is a point of interest, right?"

She smiled. It was a weak one, but she was getting her control back. "Yes, there is a church at the top of his street. Did you see the name of it when we were there?"

I was pressing icons on the screen, so I didn't answer right away. When I finally hit one of the choices, I looked up at her. "No. But there are only three churches in this part of town. We know the name of the one on the harbor so we can ignore that. I checked, and the other is too far away to be the right one. I've keyed in the location and the route is ready. Let's go."

WE MADE it to the church in record time. It seemed like all this running around was starting to make me fit, because despite the limp, I was hardly panting at all when we stopped. Lu was fully in control again and I could tell by the set of her shoulders that she was ready to do whatever it took to get Matthieu back.

"That's Marran's house," Lu said, pointing to the door. "What do you think we should do now?"

"I've been giving that some thought. I don't think knocking on the door and asking if they have Matthieu is a good idea." I turned off the GPS. "I think I can find the back-way in. If we sneak around there, we might hear something that will lead us to Matthieu."

Lu glanced around the street. "I guess it's as good an idea as any. It's too busy now to try going through the front. How do we get into that warren of streets behind the house?"

I led her down to where Matthieu had parked the car earlier. Lu was right. I'd hardly noticed that the street was full of pedestrians when we stopped. Shutters were open for the first time since we'd been up here. I saw some of the windows looked into shops, or rather workspaces. We passed a drug store, a watch repair place, and a lawyer's office. There was a life to the street that made it seem so much less sinister than earlier.

"The alley is along here." I pointed to a break in the walls around the houses. "It's hard to get lost on the way up. Matthieu and I came this way when we were looking for you."

The gardens were deserted, so we were able to hurry back to Marran's door without worrying that we would be seen. We arrived, and after a glance around, we snuck through the gate into his yard. No one was in the kitchen. No one in sight through the window.

"Do we just walk in? I don't think he's the kind of man who would let us do that without repercussions." Lu was looking through the window as she spoke.

"Well, we're standing in his backyard, so I think we've already crossed a line." I checked the door. It was off the latch. "I'll just go in and have a quick look. Maybe no one is home. You stay here just in case."

"Be careful." She stepped away from the window and stood against the wall. "I'm starting to think this is a very bad idea."

"Try calling Matthieu again. I'll be two minutes." I slipped through the door as Lu dug in her purse for the phone.

The house felt empty, but it couldn't be, the door was left open. Then again, maybe Marran was such a badass that he didn't need to worry about break-ins.

I heard a radio playing upstairs, pop music. I stepped from the kitchen to the hall and paused to listen. No sound that indicated people were there. I walked the length of the hallway to the front room. No one was inside. If anyone was home, they were upstairs. I glanced around but there was no note saying 'we've got the copper' or anything resembling a crate of guns. Too much time had passed, so I turned to go. Then I heard a phone ring — a cell phone with a familiar tone. A quiet rendition of RESPECT by Aretha Franklin. It was Matthieu's phone.

I followed the sound and found his cell down the side of the sofa. Grabbing it, I hurried out to the garden in case someone had heard it and was coming to investigate.

I pulled Lu along with me back into the alley. "He was there." I held out the phone as evidence.

She paled, and I saw tears start to form on her eyelashes. Then she swallowed and took control of herself again. "Sorry, I know I can't breakdown right now. I'm just... How are we going to find him?"

I had only two ideas. "I think we should go to the police. If we can get them to investigate, it will be better."

"They haven't been that eager up to now," she said. "But you're right, we probably should try. What if they won't help?"

That was idea number two. "We need to go back to the warehouse we found. If Marran has Matthieu, I think that's the best place to start."

TWENTY-FOUR

After waiting for an hour to get someone at the station to find anyone who was free to help us, we were sitting in the office of the Colonel himself. In my mind, it was confirmation of how corrupt the Colonel was that no one seemed to think a missing gendarme was important enough to drop what they were doing to help find him.

The Colonel was explaining that there was little evidence that Marran had kidnapped Matthieu. "It has not been long enough to consider him a missing person."

"I don't know why you are protecting Arnaud Marran, but I think you would at least want to seem to be interested in stopping criminals." I had lost my tact about ten minutes ago. "We found his cell phone in Marran's house. We know he was going to confront Marran about Audrey Wylie. We told you we found her locked up in an abandoned house. She can confirm who kidnapped her."

"Yes, I understand." The Colonel shifted papers on his desk. "We will send someone to interview Madame Wylie, and if she has useful information, we will act on it. As to protecting Arnaud Marran, you should not make accusations that have no basis. I will overlook your admission that you trespassed on his property. If he does not choose to press charges, we will leave it there."

"I see. But you are not going to look for Matthieu?" Lu asked. "I'm surprised that you don't value your men enough to make an effort. How long before we can report him missing?"

The Colonel was taken aback for a second by the ice princess in her voice. "It is generally three days before an adult is considered missing. People have private lives, ladies. Perhaps Matthieu will be found with one of his women. Ah, I see you did not know of his reputation as a Lothario."

I thought that was laying on one too many handfuls of bull-shit. He should have waited for us to react to that before observing we were surprised. Perhaps other people believed his act, but I was getting ready to assault him. Only the thought that Lu would be left alone to find Matthieu stopped me slapping the smile off the Colonel's face.

Lu sniffed and said, "And if that is not the case, perhaps you will regret not acting sooner."

The Colonel straightened and seemed to gather his authority around him in reaction to Lu's challenge. "I think it's time for you to leave. May I suggest that you stop this investigating now that Madame Wylie is safe? Your holiday is, perhaps, ready to begin. I think you will enjoy the Loire valley."

We stood, and the Colonel held out his hand to shake. I just looked at him and turned to the door. Lu was already there yanking it open.

When we stepped into the hall again, I saw Dominique hurry back to her station at reception. "What the hell was she doing?" I didn't wait for a reply but strode over to the reception desk.

Before I could ask if she'd been listening, she said, "I understand that Matthieu is missing and you think Arnaud Marran is involved."

"So, you were listening?"

She nodded. "I am not ashamed of this. I have some information for you. Wait in those seats."

I beckoned Lu, and we waited as commanded. "I feel like I'm sitting outside the principal's office," I whispered.

"I know. I thought she hated us," Lu said. "But then, maybe, it's just her Frenchness. Perhaps she's just snobby to every foreigner."

"I think she likes Matthieu more than she hates us. I think it's more likely about jealousy of you than a general hatred of foreigners."

Dominique came back from the printer room with a sheet of paper and returned to her desk. When she sat, she curled her finger to call me to the desk. "Oh, my god, she's crazy." I turned to Lu and rolled my eyes before obeying the order.

"I require your signature on this document," she said in a loud voice. Sliding a form toward me, she folded the printout into four and pushed it under the official document.

I scribbled a signature on the line and palmed the printout. "You may go now." She turned away and started typing.

Lu joined me, and we walked to the street. I wanted to be far away from the station before I looked at the paper so there was no chance for anyone to notice. I figured if she needed to be that sneaky, either Dominique was a conspiracy nut, or there was good reason to be secretive. I voted for option number two.

A block away, Lu pulled me to a stop. "What was that all about?"

I unfolded the printout and stared at it. "It's a list of addresses. I think these are places owned by Arnaud Marran."

There were five addresses on the list. I crossed out the first one, Marran's home address. We didn't need to go back there.

"Any idea where these others are?" I pointed to the remaining addresses, hoping that she'd seen more of the town on her dates with Matthieu.

"No. I don't think standing here is the best place to figure it out. I need something to keep me going. Let's get some coffee."

My stomach rumbled. "And lunch, something quick."

We sat at one of the small tables at a nearby bistro, ordered a pizza to share, and a glass of wine each. I made another promise to my liver that it could rest when I got home.

"Get the GPS out," Lu said, taking the list from me. "We can plot out routes and then read the directions before we start out. Then we can go to them in order. I bet one of these is the warehouse, and maybe one is the house where you found Audrey."

"Oh, yeah that reminds me. I gave Audrey my key so she could go home when the doctor checked her out. So, don't ditch me."

I turned on the GPS and waited for it to get a satellite signal. Our pizza arrived while it was searching. I slid a piece from the plate and folded it like I'd seen on movies set in New York. It was actually helpful, leaving me with a free hand to enter information in the GPS. "Give me the addresses, and I'll put them in as favorites. Then we can check the directions. Give me the crossed off one too. It might be important to find our way between the others and Marran's home."

Lu read from the printout between bites of pizza.

"Slow down. We don't want you getting cramps from shoving food down your throat. We're going to be moving pretty fast." I dug in my purse and swallowed one of the pain killers the doctor had given me. I didn't want to handicap us with limping if I could avoid it.

I double checked the locations by route instructions when the addresses were entered. We had the warehouse, Marran's home, and three other locations. The house where I found Audrey was not on the list, because none of the directions took us near the cemetery. "Three places to check. Do you have a preference?"

"No, well... Maybe we should try the ones we don't know about first. If Marran knows we've identified the warehouse it's unlikely he will take Matthieu there. And I haven't a clue how we'll get through that door."

I planned the route to the first unknown address. "It's not that far. Get the bill and I'll see about a route to the other address." According to the GPS it was five minutes to the first house and fifteen from there to the next. If we walked fast, we might cut the time in half.

LOCATION NUMBER one was a small house across from Saint Philippe's church. The house stood in the center of a walled garden. All the shutters were open, children played in the garden, and two middle aged women were monitoring the activity.

"I guess every bad guy does some good. It's not likely to be where they are keeping Matthieu." We walked away from the daycare toward the second address.

"Do you think we'll find Matthieu alive?" Lu asked in a small voice.

"They kept Audrey alive and well for all those days. I don't think they will do anything to Matthieu unless they have to. He's a cop, Lu. No matter how corrupt the Colonel is, they are going to be wary about hurting a cop." I tried to believe it myself. I didn't like to see Lu this worried.

"I wondered about that," she said. "Why do you think they did that? Keep Audrey alive, I mean."

I leaned against the wall. "It puzzled me too. While the

doctor was patching me up, Audrey gave me her theory. She thinks they were waiting for permission to do something. Apparently, whoever buys their guns is powerful enough to make them leery of doing something rash – although taking her was pretty rash. Marran took Audrey without letting this customer know. He needed to make sure that dealing with Audrey would not cause more problems. She'd overheard them discussing sending her with one of the shipments. Russia was mentioned."

Lu sped up a little. "So, it seems he did the same thing with Matthieu. I guess that makes me feel better. But, Charity, I need to find him today. Okay?"

I patted her arm. "That's the plan. We are going to find him. I won't let this go wrong."

She smiled at me, and I saw the effort it took for her to do it. She kept talking, "I may not come to Paris with you. When we find Matthieu, I'm going to stay here. If he wants me to, I'll move here."

"I already guessed you were planning to stay and not come home with me. But you should come to Paris. Matthieu will need a real break, and Paris is very romantic." I wasn't ready to give up my best friend just yet.

"That's true. Maybe a little pre-nuptial honeymoon. And, don't worry, I will come home with you. I don't know if Matthieu will want me to just stay. It's just a holiday fling... maybe. But, if it's not, I will pack up and come back here."

I didn't pursue the pre-nuptial thing. She wrapped her arm around mine and we walked the rest of the way talking about what we'd do when this was over.

Location number two was the last of a row of houses. I told Lu to wait as I walked past. The shutters on the first floor were closed. The top floor windows were open with a flutter of lace curtain drawn out by the wind. I walked back to Lu. "Let's see if we can go around the back. This is a good candidate for holding a prisoner. The street is short and quiet. There is a lot of privacy. And if they brought Matthieu by car, they could just park by this alley, and take him through the back door. It's interesting that all of Marran's places have back door access, since it's so unusual. I guess an escape route is essential for him."

In a few seconds, we were standing at the garden gate, and I was getting worried that we were looking suspicious. "Take a look and then we keep walking. We need to do this smart. If Marran is looking out the window, he'll have already figured out why we're here. But on the off chance he hasn't, let's keep him from noticing us."

TWENTY-FIVE

As we passed the back door, I caught a glimpse of Marran leaving the kitchen. I don't think he saw us, mainly because we were still alive.

"Did you see that?" Lu asked, poking my arm. "Now, what's your plan to get inside and find out if Matthieu is there?"

Good question. I couldn't see any other vantage point where we'd be able to look into the rest of the house. The way they built residences here was great for dealing with the hot weather, but the thick walls and small rooms made them far too private for our use. I preferred open layout and big windows. Of course, that would make us more visible, so throw in a couple of tall shrubs for hiding behind. A bare yard was useless for sneaking up.

"Keep going." I tugged on Lu's arm. "We can't see into the house. We'll have to find a way to get Marran out without him locking up the on the way."

We were now halfway up the alley and running out of places to go. It didn't continue through to the next street, but dead ended in what looked like a schoolyard. "We can stand here and pretend to look at the scenery." I knew how lame that was, but I didn't want to go back past Marran's just yet. At least, we were out of his line of sight. "Do you have any ideas about how to get him out of there?"

Lu shook her head. "Is it always like this? Investigating?"

"If you mean trying to control chaos and making plans on the run, then yes, sometimes. It's different when the case is simple. I can schedule out the work and pretty much get it done with no problems. But stuff like this, it's hard to plan when the information keeps shifting on you." I took a good look at Lu. She'd been getting more down as time passed. I couldn't blame her. If it had been Jake in there, I would be storming the house and taking my chances. Even so, she looked better than she sounded. There was color in her cheeks, and a hint of steel in her expression.

She turned to glance back to the house. "What if you go knocking on the front door, and I go in the back?"

"Not a bad plan C. But it might be better to call the cops than use plan C." I had to say it, but I didn't have to sound enthusiastic.

Lu snorted. "Yeah and then we can set up our tents here so we can be comfortable while we wait. I don't think we have time to do this the official way."

"Lu, I don't think Marran is going to kill Matthieu. If he had to get permission to deal with Audrey, I don't think he'll just make a cop disappear without checking up the line of command." I turned to lean my back against the stone. It was warm from the sun, and smooth. I let the comfort soothe the tension away. I needed calm to plan. "We could wait until he leaves."

Lu started to speak, but I cut her off. "No, that's plan B and we need a plan A. One that has us all getting out alive. I want this over with as much as you do. We'll make it happen."

We were silent for a few minutes. I don't know what Lu was

doing, but I was thinking through the last few hours. Going over what we'd done. It felt like we'd waited forever to figure out what was happening, but now everything came to a head today. Audrey was safe, even if Matthieu wasn't. At least we could call Delores tonight and pass on the good news. That's it! I grabbed my purse and started digging through it.

"What are you looking for?" Lu asked as I passed her some of the larger pieces in my bag.

"Matthieu's phone."

"I have it." She handed back my stuff and pulled his cell out of her own purse. "Why?"

"Don't you remember? Marran called him."

"So?"

"We have Marran's phone number. We can call him, get him to leave, then go in and see what's happening."

AFTER TALKING IT OVER, we decided that Lu would make the call. She was better at acting than I was. She would pretend to be calling from a Russian colleague. The story was, the man was in town, and looking for Marran.

"Okay, we only need five minutes," I said. "If these houses are similar to the one they had Audrey in, we should be able to get into the front room, check out what's going on, and then find a place to hide in the house if we need to."

Lu used her own phone to dial the number we found on Matthieu's. I put my ear next to hers so I could hear everything.

"Marran."

"Mr. Marran, I am here with your Russian friend. We were expecting you to meet with us about the Canadian woman."

"*Merde*, why did I not know you were coming?"

"I do not know. And that is not our problem. Where can we meet?"

I was impressed with Lu's hidden talents. It seemed that Marran did not yet know that we had rescued Audrey.

"I am at the drop off house."

"Wait." Lu half-covered the phone and made noises like there was a conversation going on. I did my best to mutter in a man's register. "No. We do not wish to meet there. It is too much of a risk."

I heard mumbling on the other end. Lu shrugged and waited.

"There is a bar on *Rue Michel*, near the fountain. Do you know it?"

Lu turned and said, "Do you know a bar on Rue Michel?" She covered the mouthpiece for a second then said into the phone. "Very well, we will expect you to be there when we arrive." She snapped the phone shut on Marran's reply.

"That should get us more than five minutes," she said.

We went back to the mouth of the alley and peeked over the wall. I thanked whoever decided a town should have these high walls because unlike the yard, they afforded us all the privacy we needed. The back door remained open, but a flash of light from the hall preceded a slamming door.

"Let's go," I said.

We slipped through the gate, across the yard, and into the kitchen. There was no sound coming from the house, but I made Lu stay behind me as we crept down the hall toward the living room, just in case. The house looked like it hadn't been cared for in years. A shadow of mildew crept up the walls and I could see a hole in the ceiling. When we got to the opening to the room, I noticed the door was gone, another sign that the house was not tenanted.

I motioned for Lu to stay where she was, standing with her back pressed against the dusty wallpaper. Then I bent low to peek into the room. Low enough that I wouldn't immediately come into the line of sight of anyone there, high enough to be able to see what was in there. In middle of the room, facing the fireplace, back to the door, was Matthieu. He was tied to a chair and gagged, but looked okay, at least from the back.

I started to slip into the room only to stop. Walking across my line of sight, with her back to me, was Odette Pilon.

I stopped breathing, then I shifted my weight, so I moved back into the hall. When I was clear, I stood and put my fingers to my lips. Lu nodded and waited while I looked around us. There was no convenient linen closet. Only the stairs seemed to offer a place to hide and still see the action. They turned after a half flight.

I pointed her up to the landing. We would be out of sight of anyone who was on the main floor, but still be able to hear normal conversation. Of course, we'd be in trouble if anyone decided they needed something from the second floor. But we had enough trouble right now. I didn't see the point of borrowing any from the future.

I whispered what I'd seen, and then we settled on a stair, looking around the turn just as the front door slammed open.

This was going to be interesting. They had no reason to speak English and neither of us spoke French. Lu was digging into her purse again and pulling out a French English dictionary.

I raised an eyebrow, but she mouthed, "Best we have."

Marran stormed into the living room. *"Merde. Quelqu'un nous joue un tour."*

Lu looked at her book and then back at me. "Well, maybe they'll slow down. All I know is that sounds like he's pissed."

TWENTY-SIX

They were arguing loudly now in French. I turned to Lu and whispered, "He seems pissed at her, not just pissed in general. I wonder if Odette was the one who took Matthieu. That would explain a lot."

Lu was flipping through the dictionary again, trying to find a word or two we could decipher. "Yes, I had been wondering why someone who seems so in control as Arnaud Marran would do something as stupid as start kidnapping people."

The shouting from the living room was getting angrier with every word. Then a sudden bang happened, and then silence. It wasn't a gunshot, but something big had hit the floor. When the argument continued, I said, "Maybe they'll take this outside. If we get even a few minutes, we can release Matthieu and get onto the street. Or the alley, I guess."

We listened but couldn't make out any of the words now they were in full war cry. "At least they won't be looking for anyone in the house," I said. "We can probably stay here for as long as it takes."

"Or as long as it takes for one of us to start sneezing from the dust and mold." Lu leaned around the wall to peek again. "They might be able to keep this up for hours."

We listened for a while, but Lu was right we couldn't stay here indefinitely. I needed to use the bathroom already.

I thought through our options, and the tension started building in my shoulders and stomach. "Marran came back awfully quick. I expected him to be more like twenty minutes than five. He realized the call wasn't real way too soon."

Lu didn't turn to me, her concentration on the hall below. "You think the Russians called for real?"

"No. They wouldn't be fighting here if the Russians were on their way." I hoped I was right. If the Russian mob was on their way, Matthieu would be dead within ten minutes of their arrival, and we'd probably join him before the hour was out. Everything I had found out about them said they didn't leave loose ends, so it was probably going to go badly for Marran and Odette too.

"*Sortir!*" Marran shouted the word.

"He just told her to get out," Lu said. "Maybe we'll get a chance to pull Matthieu to safety soon."

Odette's voice came clearly through the sudden silence. "*Peut-être je vais appeler les Russes.*"

I looked at Lu, but she shrugged. "Something about calling the Russians."

That was not going to be a good outcome. I started to rise. "We need to do something before they are on their way."

We used the cover of the argument to make our way back to the doorway. I pointed toward the kitchen for Lu to stay safe while I scoped out the situation in the living room.

I went low again, and when I popped my head around the corner, I looked straight into the blue eyes of Matthieu Durand. He blinked and then flicked a glance at the two combatants.

They were paying no attention so he looked back at me and jerked his head to indicate I should get out of there.

I shook my head and moved back to the hall. Lu, who had not retreated to safety, looked at me for information.

I moved close to her ear and breathed the words barely at a whisper, "Matthieu is on the floor. The bang we heard must have been his chair falling."

I pointed to the kitchen and, this time, she started walking.

When we were far enough away from the living room, I started talking quietly. "They can't go on much longer. We have to do something."

"Did he look okay?" Lu asked.

"Yes, he looked fine. He seems to think we'd be better off leaving."

"But we aren't, right?"

"I think you should go to the police. Talk to Dominique, I'm sure she'll find someone to help, even if it's only in hope that Matthieu will be grateful for the rescue and fall in love with her on the spot."

Lu dug around for her phone. When she had it, she said, "I'll keep this on while I go. Turn yours off so it won't give you away. Getting the cops is going to take a while. What are you going to do?"

I listened to the argument for a second before answering. They seemed to be running out of anger, or energy. "I'm going to distract them while you get the cops. If I can get Matthieu out, we'll find you. But you need to get away from here."

Lu swallowed. I could see the wheels turning in her mind. Then I watched the decision she made to cooperate in the hardening of her face. "Be careful, Charity. It's been kind of an adventure up to now, but I just realized it could become... well, I guess I don't want to lose you or Matthieu."

I saw tears forming again in her eyes, and suddenly my own

were a bit blurry. I swallowed and turned her toward the door. "You are not going to lose anyone. Go bring the cavalry."

She turned back. "I need something first."

I rolled my eyes. "What? You need to get going. I can't start until you are on your way to the cops."

"I need the GPS. I have no idea how to get to the police station."

I swore and dug the GPS out of my purse. "Don't turn it on until you're on the street. I'm not sure how much battery life it has, and I don't want it suddenly giving directions when you are sneaking out."

I waited until Lu disappeared from sight, keeping my ears focused on the noise coming from the living room. The voice was now mostly Marran's with the occasional whine from Odette. I didn't have anything I could use as a weapon, so I was going to have to rely on my wits – sometimes it works better that way.

I crept back along the hall, wanting to surprise them. If their voices were any indication, they were wound pretty tight. If I took them off kilter, it might make the difference between getting away and getting dead. I hoped that difference would be in my favor; today was not a good day to have my luck run out.

"*Vous êtes une idiote,*" Marran said as I stepped into the room. He was talking to Odette, his back to the door.

Instead of answering, Odette stared at me. As her eyes widened Marran must have realize she wasn't reacting to his words. He started to turn, and I pasted a grin on my face.

"Good afternoon," I said. "I wasn't expecting to find you here."

A frown crossed his face as he looked me up and down. I didn't let any sign show that I was intimidated. Odette got her sense back first and launched herself at me. Marran grabbed her arm as she passed and jerked her back. "Don't make it worse."

"She has been the problem, not me." Odette tried to extract herself from Marran's grasp, but he just pulled, and she almost fell as she moved behind him. "Arnaud, please. We were fine until she came along. We were—"

"Shut up," he said, pushing her into a chair. Keeping his eyes on me, he continued to talk to Odette. "We were fine until you took the Wylie woman captive. We were successful, and the Russians trusted us. Now, I do not know if we will survive your stupidity."

Odette opened her mouth to respond but Marran spun to stare at her. She closed her mouth and crossed her arms over her chest.

"Oh, I guess no one has told you," I said, taking a small step toward where Matthieu was struggling against his bonds. "Audrey Wylie is no longer a guest in that lovely house. I suppose the fact you took good care of her will go in your favor in court."

"Stay where you are." Marran jabbed a finger at me. "You think we are going to court? Don't be a fool. If we survive after our partners hear about this, there will be no court. I am protected."

I shook my head in what I hoped was a pitying gesture. "Your protection won't hold out long when Audrey starts talking to the Canadian Embassy. Or, if you don't care about them, I'm sure someone at Interpol will be interested in the guns you have."

"The guns have been shipped," Odette snarled. "There is no evidence."

Marran slapped her. She sank back into the chair, more sullen than ever.

"Maybe we can come to an arrangement," I said. I was standing next to Matthieu now. If I could get them fighting again, maybe I could undo the bindings. I could see that it was just rope, not handcuffs or those plastic zip strips.

"What kind of arrangement do you have to offer? With no guns, this is all your word against ours. We have friends here, you do not." Marran was far too confident in his connections. In my experience when push came to shove, criminals turned on each other. If his network collapsed, he'd lose the edge of fear that kept others quiet.

"Right now, Audrey is willing to say nothing about her kidnapping, and if Matthieu is willing to do the same, perhaps you'll let him go."

Marran laughed. "I see, you think we can pretend this has not happened. You are so naive."

I shrugged. "How about this, you let Matthieu go, and I will destroy the information I have about how you smuggle guns in."

"You don't have proof," Odette screamed, rising from the chair.

"I do," I said calmly. Then I bent to remove the gag from Matthieu's mouth. "Is that better?"

He nodded but didn't answer, just swallowed, and licked his lips.

Marran had stopped Odette again in her fury to attack. He pushed her back into the chair then turned to me. "I find it very hard to believe that you have figured out how to prove this thing that has baffled the gendarmes for years. How did you get this proof? Did someone talk?" He glanced at Odette.

I wasn't sure if he meant that she had talked, or if he was making sure she wasn't getting ready to launch another attack. "I have the proof. I will tell you what it is if we have a deal."

"Why should I believe you when you say no one will go to the authorities?"

Was this a stalling tactic, or had I found the key to a deal?

"The same way I can believe you that we won't regret agreeing. We have to trust each other."

"I am not in the habit of trusting people." He waved a hand in Odette's direction. "Look at what happens when I trust someone. They do stupid things that put us all in danger."

If Odette could have, I believe she would be burning holes in Marran's back with her glare. I guess all the things he said when he was yelling didn't mean anything. But when he was quiet and rational, there was no doubt how serious he was.

Then suddenly her eyes narrowed, and she asked, "Where is your friend?"

Crap. I had hoped no one would ask. "She is searching elsewhere for Matthieu."

"Leave her out of this, Marran," Matthieu said. "Let them both go. This is between you and me. Leave the women out of it, all of them."

Marran looked at me and said, "Untie him. I don't think he will be able to do any damage. Let us talk like businesspeople. Leave the emotions out of it, yes?"

I nodded and bent to untie the ropes. As I did, I watched Marran settle into a second chair. He pulled out a cigarette and lit it. I glanced at Odette; her face was as red as her hair. I didn't envy him having to deal with her after this was over.

There were no other chairs, so when Matthieu was free, we stood waiting for the next move. I was happy to let Marran delay us.

More time for Lu to bring the French equivalent of the cavalry.

TWENTY-SEVEN

"Let us discuss how this deal will work," Marran said. His words were punctuated by puffs of smoke.

"Why don't we just all leave the house, and then it's done." I looked at Matthieu. "Lu and I will be heading out of town anyway. Audrey is inclined to get on with her life, and Matthieu, well, I don't want to speak for him."

Marran nodded as if he was considering the logic of my offer. I didn't believe it would be this easy, but I kept reminding myself that stalling for time was the plan, not getting away. Whatever I had to say to keep him from killing us was fair play. What we really intended to do was another thing.

Matthieu straightened his jacket before speaking. "You have control of the Colonel. What can I do against you in that circumstance?"

"Oh, I don't think you will stop, Durand. I have had control of the Colonel since... well he was not a colonel when we became partners. Why would I believe that you would honor your word? You have ignored his orders up to now. After all, that is why you are in this predicament, yes?"

It occurred to me that Marran might be stalling too. My

stomach sank with the thought that he was waiting for his Russian gang members, but then I remembered the real fear in his voice earlier when he mentioned them. Whatever he was up to, it didn't involve his partners.

Matthieu gave that shoulder rolling shrug and said, "Perhaps I am getting tired of this tilting at windmills."

Marran laughed, a genuine sound of amusement. "If only I could believe that, Durand. We could make a lot of money together, you and me. I am becoming very tired of dealing with stupidity and emotions in my colleagues."

I watched Odette turn white, her fury doused as she heard the contempt in Marran's voice. She looked down at her hands and unclenched them. When she looked up again, her eyes met mine, but there was no connection. Something had died inside her. I realized that she was more dangerous now than when she was at full boil.

"I think I would prefer to retire rather than start a new business, but thank you for the offer," Matthieu said as he shifted closer to me.

Marran flicked his cigarette butt into the fireplace. "I am still not a trusting man. What can you give me as assurance that this is over?" He leaned forward, resting his elbows on his legs and his chin on his clasped hands, a classic listening pose.

Before anyone could speak, Odette rose and moved to stand beside Marran. "I am sorry, Arnaud. You are right. I should not have acted so thoughtlessly. I am willing to ensure we are finished with this."

He looked up at her. The expression on his face one of amused patience, as though Odette was a puppy who had finally learned a trick. "And how will you do that, my dear?"

She flicked a glance at us, and then placed her hand on his shoulder. "Tie them up again. Then I can go and find the

Chinese bitch, and that Wylie woman. A little night trip out to the deep water and we have no evidence of foul play."

Marran reached up and patted her hand.

"Ah, child, so impetuous even when you think you are being cautious. You truly believe that you can accomplish this without being caught." His voice was gentle, and Odette smiled. I wondered how she could be so fooled. Didn't she hear that menace in his voice?

"I can. You know I can," she said it like it was a seduction. This was the weirdest conversation I'd ever witnessed.

Matthieu touched my hand, and when I looked at him, he flicked his eyes to the door. I shook my head. We had to stay until the cops came. I had no doubt that Dominique would find someone to help. It was just a matter of staying alive until they came.

I looked back at Marran. He rose from the chair and turned to face Odette. Apparently, he didn't think we were a threat, at least for the moment.

"Tell me how you will accomplish this." He took her by the shoulders and turned her so that he could see us and still watch her reaction. It meant we could see it too. He was putting on a show, and Odette had no idea he was leading her somewhere.

Her cheeks were slightly flushed. She had forgotten her rage and fear and was now warmed by his attention. Odette believed she was back in his good graces. "I will simply put them in the van to take them to the harbor. I do not understand why you are asking."

I saw his lips compress for a second before he spoke. Despite the fact that she was a vicious criminal, I suddenly felt sorry for Odette.

"You stupid bitch." He spat the words in her face and then caressed her cheek. His action and words so incompatible it sent chills through me. I heard Matthieu take in a quick breath and felt him tense.

Marran continued, "I should have known you were not capable of rational thought. If you had not been so stupid, I would have enough money to buy myself companions who could think beyond their next fuck. You are just like your *salope* mother."

"Arnaud, please..."

He pushed her away and she fell into the fireplace, her elbow connecting with the stone of the hearth. I felt faint when I heard the joint crack, but she was too far gone to notice pain.

Marran snarled at her. "Don't beg. I should have known better than to get involved with you. Your family is useless and the sooner you are all gone the better for us."

Odette reached out a hand as though touching Marran would change the way he was looking at her. "Tell me what I have to do. *Je suis désolée. S'il vous plaît, ne faites pas ça.*"

He slapped her hand away. "Do not touch me again." When she cowered away, he turned to us and said, "You see how I am burdened by stupidity? I truly believe she would have not realized she couldn't move you by herself until she pulled up the van tonight. Perhaps I should have let her try, no? And then I could have called our esteemed Colonel to do his job. Well his official job, anyway."

I almost answered him before I realized he was taunting Odette. I wasn't going to help him destroy her. But he didn't wait for an answer. Turning back to her, he shouted something in French, speaking so fast I couldn't make out any of the words.

Matthieu nudged me again. "Let's go. We can sort this out later."

I kept my eyes on the fight in front of me, fascinated by the way Odette changed from second to second. Her cringing demeanor had vanished like cigarette smoke, and she was screaming back at Marran. She wasn't paying attention to us any longer, neither was Marran. I got the sudden feeling this was a mating dance and he was enjoying the stimulation. He wasn't yelling. It was creepy, like he was absorbing all her rage.

Since he seemed to have forgotten us, I figured we could talk, quietly. "No, we need to stay. Lu is bringing help. If we go, Odette and Marran might leave, and then we have nothing."

"We have our lives. Do you think this is safe? It is not." He nudged me toward the door.

"Just a few more minutes, Matthieu. We need to make sure this ends." I wasn't happy about being here either, but we had to give the cops a chance to get here.

"No, we go now." He put his hand in the small of my back.

I looked at the two combatants, and then changed my mind. Even if Lu arrived with the cops, they wouldn't be able to do anything to stop Marran in the long run. I nodded and took Matthieu's hand before I moved toward the door. I wasn't going to let him stay behind and play the hero. If he was hurt, Lu would kill me.

I took three steps before Odette noticed us. I'd taken my eyes off them to concentrate on getting through the door without making any noise. But suddenly the shouting stopped. Only Marran's controlled voice sounded.

Then Odette screamed out, "*Non!* Stop!"

I spun to see what she was going to do to make us stop, but Matthieu pulled me behind him. I peeked over his shoulder and I saw Odette reach to push Marran out of her way. Caught by surprise, Marran twisted in her hand and Odette was halfway to us when he shouted, "Odette, *non!*"

We were only inches from the door. Matthieu took a half step backwards and I had to move to avoid being trampled. Odette kept coming, her hand raised, fist clenched.

"Charity, run," Matthieu said, barely above a whisper. "Let me deal with this."

Not a chance. I was not abandoning him to these psychos. I sidestepped so he couldn't force me to keep moving backwards.

Before Odette reached Matthieu, Marran grabbed her arm and jerked her backwards. She stumbled and he twisted aside to avoid being knocked down again. Odette ended up on her hands and knees on the dusty carpet. Her head down, she was panting like a prize fighter in round ten.

"Enough," Marran snarled at her. "Get yourself under control before I have to do it for you. I will not be coaxed out of your punishment next time. You will regret your behavior. Remember, I am in charge. You are just a soldier in this organization."

Matthieu was still intent on retreat. He took a step toward the door and wrapped his arm around my waist to drag me with him. Only two more steps and we could run for the street.

"You stop!" Marran flung a hand at us as though he could grab us and pull us back into the room. We did as ordered. He reached into his jacket with the other hand. "Thank you for confirming my belief that I cannot trust anyone. It is refreshing to be right about one's enemies, at least."

Matthieu made a calming motion with his hands. "You cannot blame us for trying to escape. You don't have faith in Mademoiselle Pilon either. Deservedly so, I think."

Marran smiled. "Oh, yes you are correct. Odette Pilon has been a fun companion, but she is not ready to be the mastermind she believes she is. I think, though, she has had one good idea, yes?"

My stomach turned. This had gone from a farce to a deadly game in a split second.

"I have not heard a good idea," Matthieu said, giving me a small push toward the door.

I didn't move. Matthieu sighed before giving up on saving me.

Marran flicked his eyes to the defeated Odette. "Oh, yes, she had a very sensible suggestion. And I believe it is time to bring this to an end."

After that last glance, he paid no attention to Odette. She struggled to her feet as he spoke, her glare no longer focused on me or Matthieu. Marran pulled a gun out of his jacket pocket and pointed it at Matthieu's head.

"Do you have any last words of wisdom?" he asked. "Perhaps you wish to tell me another lie about how I can trust you?"

I tried to think of a way to stall, just for a minute. Then I'd worry about the next minute. It was like thinking through soup. I couldn't bring up any ideas, no smart assed comments, and no rational argument. All that kept running through my brain was *think of something, stupid*. I was going to get Matthieu killed because I didn't leave when he first said we should go. If I survived, the guilt would kill me.

I ignored the voice in my head and kept trying to think of a way to slow Marran down.

Matthieu didn't seem to have any problem acting, because he stepped toward Marran and said, "Now, Arnaud, you are the one who is going to make things worse. I think a couple of gunshots will bring attention that you will not be able to avoid. Put the gun down and let us talk again."

Marran snorted. "I will be gone before that attention is a problem."

I was frozen in place, but Matthieu took a step closer. "And what about Odette? Do you think she will take the blame for killing us? Do you think, perhaps, she will be angry enough to start talking?"

Marran glanced at Odette and dismissed her with a flick of his free hand. "She will do as she is told."

I reached to pull Matthieu back to me. He was too close. If Marran decided to shoot, there was no way Matthieu would survive. He swatted my hand away from his jacket keeping his attention on the gun.

"This is something you will regret," Matthieu said, taking another step forward. I told myself he had training, and he knew what he was doing, but all I could hear in my mind was Lu crying when her husband died. I couldn't allow Matthieu to be the reason she broke down again.

"I think I am already regretting what has happened. Killing you will only bring an end to the problems. Killing Odette, well I have been meaning to do that for some time now."

When he said that, Odette jerked as though he had slapped her. Then, a scream forming on her lips, she lunged at him. He fell as she spun him around. Odette landed on top and raised her hand fingers clawed. The scream finally came out of her, an inhuman noise of pain and anger. She lowered her hand, going for his eyes.

I tried to shout, but any sound I got out was drowned in the shot Marran fired. Odette jerked back, a blossom of red growing on her shirt, just below her breasts.

TWENTY-EIGHT

The sound of the shot was still burning my ears as Matthieu dashed toward Odette. Marran struggled to his feet, holding the gun loosely. I watched Matthieu slap the gun out of Marran's hand into the corner of the room as he reached for Odette. The man was in shock, he didn't react at all to the loss of his gun.

"Charity, call an ambulance," Matthieu ordered. "Tell them to come to *Le Maison Verte*."

My purse had hit the floor when the gun went off. I bent to grab it and pull out the phone. "What number do I dial?"

"One one two," Matthieu said as he pulled off his jacket and rolled it into a ball. "Tell them what happened."

I kept my eyes on Marran as I pressed the numbers. He was staring at the gun, which had fallen only a few feet away. As the operator answered, I walked over and put my foot on the weapon. I gave the operator the details. Marran gained his senses. With one look at Matthieu who was pressing his jacket against the wound, Marran moved to the door. I didn't stop him. We had enough evidence to catch him later. Even if Odette wouldn't, or couldn't, tell what happened, the blood on his hands and the fingerprints on the gun were going to send him away for a very long time.

As soon as he was gone, I kicked the gun under the couch and bent to help Matthieu. He was speaking softly in French, so I took Odette's hand and gave it a gentle squeeze. No matter what she'd done, or how crazy she was, she didn't deserve to die like this.

I was still on the line with the emergency operator and she told me the ambulance was minutes away. "And the police?" I asked.

"They will arrive," she said. "Is there any danger?"

I looked around. "No. It's all safe now."

"Then you need to let the ambulance team in the door."

I gave Odette's hand another squeeze before I ran to the front door. Marran had bolted it when he came in after our fake call. I turned the lock and tugged the door open. The emergency team was running from the van when I looked out.

The paramedics took over from Matthieu. He came toward me looking at his hands. They were covered in blood. "I think she is too far gone," he said.

I didn't know what to say. I thought that it might be better if she went, but I couldn't say it. I took his arm and drew him toward the kitchen. "We should get out of their way. When the paramedics go, we'll get the gun."

As we stepped into the kitchen, three people came in the back door. Lu took one look at Matthieu and ran to him, pulling his hands away to see the source of the blood. "What happened? Are you hurt?"

He told her the facts and turned to the two gendarmes who waited behind Lu. "Marran shot Odette Pilon. It seems she was involved in two kidnappings, Audrey Wylie, and me." He looked at the young cop and continued, "Alain, wait for the emergency team to leave, and then go and find the evidence we will need to put him away."

I recognized Alain as the gendarme who'd stayed with us when we searched Audrey's house. If I had only known he was a friend, I might have told him sooner about what we had found.

Matthieu turned back to me and Lu before speaking again, "Let's wait in the garden. I find myself in need of some sunshine and fresh air."

I made it outside before I started shaking so badly I could barely stand. "I need to sit," I said and then I plopped down onto the warm flagstones. "It's just the adrenaline. I'll be fine. But do you have any chocolate in your purse? Sugar might help this dizziness."

Lu dug out a bag of nougat. "Here. Not chocolate, but at least it has some protein in the nuts." She turned to Matthieu. "Are you really okay?"

He kissed her cheek before answering, "I will be, Lu. I am not so much in shock as in disbelief. I cannot convince myself that this might be over."

She glanced back into the house. "Is that one of the paramedics?"

I looked up and, yes, the paramedic was standing in the doorway. He nodded to us as soon as he had our attention. "I am sorry to say that your friend did not survive the bullet wound. We will take her to the hospital. You can make the arrangements there."

"She was not our friend," I said.

Matthieu stepped forward and said, "No, but she has no family who can do this, and, I think, no real friends. I will take care of the details, thank you."

The paramedic nodded and passed Matthieu a package of wipes to clean the blood away. Then he turned to reenter the house. I pulled myself up, because the dizziness had passed, and watched him join his partner. The gurney between them was covered completely in a blue blanket. The body underneath was so small it could have been a child. Hard to believe so much fury could be contained in such a tiny person.

Opening the package and scrubbing the crusted blood off his hands, Matthieu looked at us. "I will be some time here sorting out the details. Let me have Alain drive you home. We can meet at the station later."

I didn't see any reason for us to stay, so I didn't argue. I just took Lu's elbow and followed Alain out to the street. I don't think I had any fight left in me after what we'd just survived.

TWENTY-NINE

Audrey was at her house when we arrived. When she opened the door and welcomed us inside, it occurred to me that Lu and I needed to find a hotel, at least for tonight. I was not looking forward to packing and moving. I was really just looking forward to collapsing.

Audrey smiled at us and said, "Please, come in. You must be hungry." She ushered us to the dining room and poured us wine to go with what smelled like a wonderful soup.

My stomach growled, and I realized that I was starving. Along with a white bean soup, Audrey put crusty bread in front of us and a bowl of perfectly ripe plums.

"Thank you, this is perfect," Lu said. "We'll get our things out of the way as soon as we can. You'll want your home to yourself."

Audrey sat and sipped wine while we stuffed ourselves. "You can stay here until you leave for the rest of your vacation. I'll stay with Claudette. She's very anxious to get all the gritty details. I'm afraid she will be joining us for dinner later. I hope you don't mind."

"You don't have to move out for us," I said, not really

meaning it. "We can get a hotel. It will probably be a few days before we are allowed to leave anyway. Did you talk to the police?"

"Letting you stay here is the least I can do to thank you. And, no, I have not given a statement yet." Audrey took a plum and wiped off the moisture. "It seems they wish to speak to all of us at the same time. I have been commanded to bring you with me in an hour."

"We might be in for a long afternoon of answering questions and giving statements." I pushed my empty bowl aside and took a sip of the wine. It was rich and fruity, just the right balance for the slightly spicy soup.

"What time is it back home?" Lu asked. "Someone should call Delores. We haven't told her that you are safe, Audrey."

"Don't worry about that. I've already spoken to her," Audrey said. "She says thanks and to enjoy your vacation. I am sorry that so much of it was wasted finding me."

I laughed. The soup and wine doing a great job of wiping away the last hour. "Oh, I don't think it was a waste. Other than the last couple of hours, it's been really interesting getting to know all the secrets and stories of the town. Not too many tourists get to see so much detail. And I think Lu should be thanking you, not the other way around."

Lu blushed and said, "And I think I would like to freshen up before we go to the police station."

I held up my glass and said, "Go ahead. I want to finish this and then I'll get a quick shower and change when you're done." While she was out of the room, I told Audrey about Matthieu and Lu falling in love.

"Matthieu is a good man," Audrey said. "Even if this is a holiday romance, she couldn't have picked a better candidate. I wonder if he will be willing to go to Canada. I've always thought he was fighting too many stupid battles here. Perhaps we can find a way for him to work on a police exchange program? Let me think on it. I may have some connections that will help. But we should leave soon, go get ready. I'll clean up here."

I nodded, something about her made me feel like obeying. I was too tired of fighting everyone to argue anyway.

WE DROVE to the station a half hour later. I felt better for the shower; not at the top of my game, but better than I had in the garden at the house where Odette died. Lu looked fabulous. I don't really know how she managed to look so cool and elegant with so little effort. Must be a talent I didn't get when they were being handed out.

Audrey led us into the station and greeted the receptionist, "Dominique, I believe Colonel Fitzroi is expecting us."

This was the first time I'd walked in here feeling like we were going to accomplish something. Maybe we should have been more demanding and less inquiring when we arrived.

Dominique picked up the phone and pressed one button. She spoke quietly in rapid French and then ended the call. "It will be a few minutes, please wait there." She pointed at the familiar row of chairs.

This time, it really was only a few minutes before the Colonel himself came to escort us to his office. When we entered, I saw that Matthieu was already there, standing looking out the window.

"Please, let us all take our seats." The Colonel looked pointedly at Matthieu's back. "Durand, are you planning to join us?"

Matthieu turned and nodded before taking the chair next to Lu.

We sat, waiting for someone to start the conversation. I looked down the row of chairs. We were all facing the Colonel, like a gang of misbehaving school kids waiting for the principal to dole out detentions. Lu and Matthieu holding hands and looking at each other, didn't seem to mind the wait. Audrey settled back in her seat, her purse clutched firmly on her lap. I decided that waiting was the power position and turned back to face the Colonel. He was looking at papers on his desk. I crossed my arms and bit down on my lip to contain the words I was bursting to say.

The silence dragged on for two minutes; I timed it. Okay that was enough. "Is someone going to take our statement?" I asked, not willing to waste any more of my vacation on stupid power plays. "Is the evidence being tested? Are you looking for Marran?"

The Colonel sighed and sat forward in his chair. "The answer to all of your questions, Madame Deacon, is no. You are here to listen to what I have to tell you. And then I can only hope you will leave our town to the peaceful existence it had before your arrival."

That got Lu's attention. "Why not? How will you arrest Marran if you don't take our statements and get his fingerprints off the gun?"

The light was beginning to dawn for me as it had, apparently, done for Audrey before we'd arrived. I didn't let the Colonel answer, "Because they are not charging Marran with anything," I said. "Because the Colonel is still in Marran's control. He said there would be no repercussions. We are here to be told the official story."

"That is a serious allegation," The Colonel said. "You must be careful what you say."

I felt all the anger and frustration well up in my chest. "You had someone dispose of the gun, yes?" I didn't wait for his answer. "So, everything will be blamed on Odette, and Marran gets to continue on with his little empire."

The Colonel cleared his throat before answering. I told myself it was because he was embarrassed to tell us such a blatant lie. "It seems that the weapon used to kill Mademoiselle Pilon has indeed disappeared. And, yes, all of the information we have been able to collect points to her as the only culprit in this affair."

I opened my mouth to tell the Colonel exactly what I thought of his little conspiracy when Matthieu reached over and tapped my shoulder. I looked at him, and he shook his head. "Charity, it is not worth it." He turned back to face his boss. "I do have some questions, while we are here."

"I do not think your questions are necessary, Durand. Let us agree this situation is over and get on with our lives."

"Oh, but my questions are important." Matthieu stood and, for a second, I thought he was going to lean in and shout in the Colonel's face. But he simply turned and looked out the window again. "If, as you say, the case is closed, what assurances do we have that Madame Wylie will not be kidnapped again?"

"Why would someone wish to do that? Durand, you are complicating this." The Colonel flicked a glance at Audrey as he spoke. "Do not unnecessarily frighten the ladies."

Lu and I rolled our eyes. Did he think this was the 1950s? Did he forget we had tracked down a criminal, and some of us 'ladies' had almost died?

Matthieu gave me a warning look and I zipped my lips and threw away the key. He nodded and said, "I know that, Colonel. But since she was already taken once, it is possible that someone might believe she is a danger to their operations."

Matthieu was right. I was leaving, so Marran would have no reason to retaliate on me. Lu, whether she left or stayed, was safe because if she stayed, Matthieu would protect her. Audrey was going to be in danger every day without some guarantee it was over.

The Colonel pouted his lips in thought. "If she does not provoke any interest, I believe she will be safe. That is the best I can do, I am afraid. Perhaps she would be safer to move back to Canada?"

I followed Matthieu's gaze to Audrey. She was taking something from her purse. A peppermint? The lady was cool, I'll give her that. She looked up at us and smiled. "I appreciate the concern, but perhaps I can suggest a solution. I like living here so I will not be returning to Canada as you kindly suggest, Colonel. Now, let us all be honest with each other. We know about the gun running. We know the Russians are involved. And I have to admit, there is very little we can do to stop smuggling in this town. It's been going on since the first boat docked in the harbor a thousand years ago."

I gained a new understanding of what Delores told me. If Audrey was this determined to get her own way when she was fighting segregation, no wonder people shut up and listened.

She gave the Colonel a chance to refute her statement, but he was silent. "Very well. I don't like what is going on, but I am a pragmatist. Colonel Fitzroi, if anything should happen to me every piece of information that I found, and that Charity puzzled out will be sent to Interpol and to the top ten newspapers in Europe. That much attention will be difficult to dodge, and your career will be over. In fact, a prison sentence will likely be the outcome for you. As for Arnaud Marran, he believes he is a hard man, that he runs this town."

The Colonel stood. "Madame—"

Audrey leaned toward the Colonel. "If his organization is exposed, his partners will not be forgiving. I suggest you let him know that as long as I am left in peace, I will not disclose the information. If I am not in contact with a certain person daily, the information will be released."

The Colonel was ashen, and I thought he might pass out

before responding. I guess he didn't think little old ladies were worth worrying about. Then he cleared his throat and seemed to gain back some of his authority. "I find it difficult to believe you will unleash a gang war here."

She smiled at him. "Oh, but it will only happen if I am kidnapped or killed. At which point, I don't believe I will care what happens here."

She rose and we followed. "Before we leave, I have a bit of advice for you. Try to disengage Marran from the Russians, and perhaps have him smuggling something a little more benign than guns. I understand that is a very violent and unstable market."

THIRTY

When we got back to Audrey's, she packed a small overnight bag and left us to sort ourselves out for the rest of our stay. We had enough time to relax and try to let go of the events of the last day, before everyone would be back for dinner. It was going to be potluck and Audrey told us not to buy anything. Apparently, we had provided sufficient wine and chocolate for twice the people who would be there.

"I need to be in Paris in two days," I said when Lu joined me in the living room. "So, have you decided? Are you coming?"

Lu grabbed one of the chilled bottles of rosé before sitting next to me. She poured two glasses and raised hers in a toast. "Cheers! It's over. I need to talk to Matthieu before I decide anything. What are you going to do with the next two days? There is a lot of France between here and Paris."

I didn't really want to tour by myself. I could do it, but it was no fun without someone to share. Anyway, I didn't want to plan the details tonight. I just wanted to enjoy the company. "If you stay here, maybe I'll see about a couple of day trips. But don't worry about me. What's the deal with you and Matthieu?" It hurt to think I would be alone when I left. Lu had Matthieu,

Audrey had her friends. All I had was dread that I'd screwed up my relationship with Jake.

"I don't know," Lu answered, settling on the couch. "Matthieu may not feel the same."

When she said that, I knew she was lost. Her eyes shone and a blush crossed her cheeks. I hoped he would make her happy, otherwise I would keep my promise and hurt him badly. She bit her lip before continuing, "Let's wait and see after I've had a chance to talk to him. Maybe he can take some more time off and show us around."

I didn't want to talk about possibilities any longer. I wanted to focus on Paris with Jake, not on Vancouver without him, or my best friend. And I didn't want to make Lu's future decisions in any way about me. I got up and started setting the table. "I wonder what we'll be treated to tonight. You know it's odd to be looking forward to dinner without worrying how we are going to try to solve a mystery."

Lu took the silverware out of the drawer and helped me. "I know. Do you remember how to just enjoy ourselves?"

We both laughed at that. "I'm sure it will come back to us," I said grabbing a handful of napkins.

Audrey and Claudette showed up just as we put the last glass on the table. I'm not usually a big fusser about table setting, but Lu knew what was supposed to be done, and Audrey had everything we needed. It felt like more of a celebration than a normal dinner with everything looking so perfect.

Claudette placed a heavy casserole dish on the counter, and Audrey added a full grocery bag. "We have my specialty, *daube de bœuf*," Claudette said. "It is very hearty, but this is a cool evening, and we are not going dancing."

She lifted the lid of the casserole, and a rich stew aroma filled the room. My mouth started to water, and I picked up a spoon to have a taste, but Claudette slapped my hand away. "No, first we have what Audrey has contributed."

Lu took the bread and filled a wooden bowl with slices, while Audrey pulled small packets from the bag. "Get me the large blue platter please, Charity," she said. We arranged cold meat and figs on the platter. Audrey took her secret stash of tapenade and placed it in beautiful china pots in the center.

"You had that hidden pretty well," I said feeling a giggle rise. "Guy told us how fond you are of his wares."

"Don't be cheeky, Charity," Audrey said. "Guy is a married man, and much too young for me in any case."

"Come, we are almost ready," Claudette called. "Now we only wait for the handsome Matthieu to grace us with his presence."

As she finished speaking, Matthieu came through the front door, a white box in his hands.

"Dessert has arrived," he announced, then glanced at the table which was covered in food. "I hope we will have room for it. Ladies, you have enough food for an army."

"We have all night to fill," Audrey said as she took the box from him. "Sit. Let's talk and enjoy the evening."

We did as ordered. Claudette dragged out the details of the last few days, well at least as much as we would share. There were some details I was trying to forget and telling them wouldn't help me do that.

By the time Matthieu served the *daube*, we were all feeling relaxed. The heartiness of the stew just made the evening more comfortable.

"So, Matthieu, what is next for you?" Claudette asked. "Are we to lose you to this lovely lady?"

Lu blushed as she said, "We were planning to discuss this later, Claudette. Between the two of us."

Matthieu smiled and picked up his wine glass without saying anything.

"Pish, Lu, we are all friends here. If friends cannot help you sort out the future, who can?"

I kept quiet. As much as I thought Lu and Matthieu deserved their privacy, I agreed with Claudette. It affected all of us so we should be part of the discussion.

Before we could get any further, someone knocked at the front door. Matthieu waved Audrey back to her seat. "Let me. We do not know if it is Marran coming back."

It was a man by the sound of the voices. Matthieu returned with the Colonel in tow. Our visitor did not look happy, his face was grey as though he hadn't slept for a week or had just been smacked down by a little old lady.

"I will not take much of your time," the Colonel said, his eyes taking in the mess on the table and finding fault. "I have been authorized to disclose information to you." He eyed Claudette. "Perhaps you would excuse us for a few moments, Madame Lesart."

"Claudette will stay, Colonel," Audrey said, placing a hand on Claudette's arm to stop her leaving. "Say what you must, and then leave us alone to enjoy our evening."

The Colonel sighed. "Very well. I have been authorized to inform you that I was a member of an elite task force. We have been infiltrating Marran's organization for years, and your actions, this last week, have destroyed every connection we had built. If you had only been less determined to undermine me, Durand, this episode would have ended very differently."

"If you had trusted Matthieu, I'm sure he would have," I said. This jerk was not going to spoil our plans. "Besides, Audrey is safe. It seems like a good outcome."

Colonel Fitzroi looked like he was going to spit, he was so

angry. "Yes, we would have found Madame Wylie. But, have you forgotten that a woman died today?"

Shit. He had a point. "I am sorry Odette had to die."

As Matthieu stepped between us, I realize the Colonel and I were inching closer. "It is unfortunate," Matthieu said. "But, I think, not our fault. Colonel, have you finished delivering your message?"

"No," he answered. Taking control of his anger, the Colonel became all business. "Odette Pilon was not the only casualty of this disaster. An hour ago, Marran's head was discovered on the deck of *Le Canard Bleu*.

I dropped into the chair. "Do you have any suspects?

The Colonel sneered. "I think we all suspect this is the result of failing to do as the Russian Mob requires. But we have nothing that will allow us to make an arrest. Thanks to Durand, we have no evidence and no contacts. His incompetence has finally—"

"Will you be able to continue undercover?" I asked before Matthieu could respond. As much as he creeped me out, I didn't like the idea that the Colonel would have to start his investigation again.

"It is too early to know. Now, I suggest that you leave as quickly as possible. Madame Wylie, it is no longer safe for you. Durand, we can discuss your return to the force in the morning." He turned to leave.

"Colonel Fitzroi," Audrey spoke quietly, but he spun to face her as though she'd issued an order. "I am not going to leave. I told you this afternoon, I like it here."

"But I cannot promise to keep you safe, Madame."

"I am an old woman. If the Russian Mob wants to kill me, then it's only going to make a difference of a few years. And being part of a task force does not make it impossible for you to be corrupt."

"I assure you, Madame, I have resisted temptation you would not understand. I am not corrupt. You realize that this evidence of yours is no longer valid?"

Oh, that was the wrong tack. Audrey's eyes gleamed. "I am not stupid, Colonel. I am just old. I will not do anything to attract their attention. They have no reason to believe I can do them harm. The two people who could cause them problems are dead. Can you feel as secure?"

He swallowed, and I realized he must be very deep into Marran's organization. If he wasn't on the kill list, he was, at least, of interest.

"I hope you are right, Madame. Now I will leave you to your cleaning up." This time he made it to the door. "That reminds me. Please remember that your car must be parked completely in your driveway in the future." He sniffed and pulled the door open.

At the sound of the Colonel's car starting, Matthieu reached for his glass and said, "Before we discuss the future, I must tell you that I have made a decision. I am not going to ask for my job back. I am finished with the gendarmerie."

Lu glanced at me. This was going to change the options. I hoped it would change it for the better – well better for me anyway.

"Lovely," Claudette said. "Now. That means you are free to entertain Charity and Lu until they go home." She seemed oblivious to any threat.

"I should look for a new job," Matthieu said, but there was little conviction in his tone.

"Come with us to Paris," I said. "You can show us some of the country on the way. We have a couple of days before I meet Jake. It might be a good idea to get out of town anyway."

He shrugged. "It would be nice, but as Lu said, we should

discuss this later. It is something for the two of us to decide, yes?"

We changed the subject, and Lu threw me a silent thank you. Over the next two hours, we completely ignored the topics of threats, and death, and Russian Mobs while Audrey and Claudette amused us with gossip about the neighborhood and some racy stories about when Claudette was in her twenties. I was starting to think that I was going to be the most boring old lady around. Even with my job, I couldn't compete with their stories.

Dessert was an assortment of perfect little pastries that went with the espresso and brandy we took into the living room.

"We must go and get our beauty sleep," Claudette announced. "At our age, the late nights are not kind."

Audrey sighed and rose to join Claudette. "Leave the dishes, I'll clean them tomorrow."

We let them leave and then started clearing away the dishes. I was torn between wanting to stay up and help Matthieu and Lu figure out what to do and going upstairs to give them privacy to figure it out for themselves. I turned on the water and said, "I'll wash if you dry." I decided to let them tell me to give them some privacy if they wanted it.

Lu took the dish towel and Matthieu waited to put away the dishes.

"Matthieu, I think what the Colonel said changes things. You should come to Canada." Lu said. So much for diplomacy.

"You may be right," he said. "I do not wish to make such a big change based on the possibility of a threat. Let us agree on Paris but discuss Canada at another time."

"I am more than happy to have you come," I said, handing the clean platter to Lu. "I think you'll like Jake. And it will be fun to have someone show us around on the way."

Lu dried the platter and passed it to Matthieu. I had a

sudden rush of warmth. This was what a family was supposed to be like. This was the kind of thing I missed because my parents were always overseas helping others.

"And after Paris?" Matthieu asked. "Is there an after?"

I handed the last clean dish to Lu. "I think maybe it's time you had some privacy."

Lu turned to me with panic in her eyes. "No, you're my best friend. Whatever we plan is going to affect you."

Matthieu nodded. "Yes, Lu is right. This is a big decision and it involves all three of us. Open the other bottle of wine and we'll talk. I confess I will not be going home tonight so I do not worry about how much I have drunk."

I couldn't figure out why she wanted me there, but I wasn't going to argue. If he wanted my opinion, he'd get it. We settled in the living room again, and I waited for someone to speak.

Lu was more nervous than I had ever seen her before. She took a deep breath and started talking, "Matthieu, I don't think we can leave this until later. I almost lost you today, and I need to know what we are going to do. If you want me to stay here, I will. I don't care about any threats. But I think it would be better if you came with us to Canada." She held up a hand when he started to speak. "Please, let me say this. I promise I will keep my mind open."

When he nodded, she continued, "We don't know if it's safe here. If you come to Canada with us, it may not be perfect, but it is away from here."

I kept my mouth shut. Lu seemed to want me for moral support, not to boost her argument. I had a hint of what was coming.

"This is a good point. But I will need a job, and there will be a lot of paperwork to get through before I can start earning a living."

He seemed to want to say more, but I forgot my pledge to

keep quiet, "Audrey says she knows some people who could expedite whatever approvals you need. Maybe get you a consulting job with the local police."

"I think I am finished with the bureaucracy of official work," Matthieu said. "In fact, I am sure of it."

"In that case, I have an idea that might help," I said. "You know I'm a private investigator, right? Well, I think you could work with me for a while. You have everything it takes to be a good PI. And if you like it, you can get your license."

The way she turned and beamed at me, it obviously hadn't occurred to Lu, but I thought it was a great idea. I could easily drum up some more business to fill the gap.

"It is something to think about," Matthieu said. "I could, perhaps, do that here. It will be a challenge for me to make an income to support you, Lu." This time he held up a hand to stop Lu speaking. "No. I know that is not a popular attitude, but I am a little old fashioned and believe I must contribute, if not completely support the family."

And here we were. The big ugly truth. This is why Lu really wanted me here.

"You don't need to worry about supporting me, Matthieu," she said. "My husband left me well provided for."

I cringed, that was probably the worst way to put it. Matthieu drew back and a flush crossed his cheeks. Lu was not usually that blunt, it was a sign of how important Matthieu was to her, and how nervous she was.

Matthieu spoke into the tense silence, "I will not live off you. I have always made my own way and I'm not going to change that now."

Lu stiffened, and I felt a storm coming. This was going to end in a way that wouldn't be resolved in the time we had left. If they didn't get past this, they would lose each other. And

Matthieu had brought Lu back to life over the last few days. I wasn't going to let them break up.

I held up my hands for peace. "Look, it's not Lu's fault she's rich, Matthieu. And she'll be rich here as well as back home. It's not like the two of you can't change your mind and come back. This is an opportunity."

Matthieu looked at both of us. "It seems I must obey. I will learn how to get my own way at some point, Lu. Do not get used to this." He kissed her cheek and I relaxed. If they could stay focused on the way they felt about each other, we would find a way to get past any obstacle.

Relaxing into the sofa, he held up a finger for each point. "We agree, I think, that we have the problem of the proud Frenchman who needs a job, and the problem of Charity, the best friend who wants to keep Lu close. And the problem of Lu who wants everything and wants it in Canada even though she says she will be happy to stay in France."

We laughed. "Just how proud are you, Matthieu?" Lu asked. "Will you live with me, or do you need your own home? If you are willing to come to Canada, then we only have the proud Frenchman problem — proud handsome Frenchman problem — to solve. I will be happy, Charity will be happy, and I'm sure, eventually, you will be happy."

"In seriousness, I think it would be better for me to be independent for at least the first while," Matthieu said. I heard something in his tone that made me believe he had given up on the idea of staying. "You are right, I have no ties here. But I am worried that we are rushing."

The solution was right in front of us. I was getting too tired to wait for them to finish the lovey stuff. "Look, what about this? Matthieu, you must have some money saved. You can work with me on cases until you figure out if you want to be a PI. It's not a lot of work, but it should be enough. As for living arrangements,

I'll ask Jake if you can housesit for him until he gets back. He lives next door and that makes it convenient for work."

Lu raised an eyebrow and said, "Well?"

"It will take me some time to make arrangements. And I'm not going to commit to emigrating. I will consider it a long vacation. After that, well, then we will see."

THE NEXT MORNING, I was happy to see Lu and Matthieu were relaxed with each other. We had coffee on the patio, the sun was cooking the chill off the stones, and I wanted to hang onto the peace of the moment a little longer. I'd be in Paris soon, colder, busier, and little opportunity to sit back and just enjoy.

"I have some arrangements to make if I am to embark on a long absence," Matthieu said, rising from the table. "Do you plan to stay here until tomorrow? Or will you go to Avignon?"

I'd given up on any plans to see other parts of France. Perhaps next time. I looked at Lu, we hadn't discussed it. She shook her head. "I'm going to stay here and help Matthieu get ready."

"Well, that settles it," I said. "I guess I'll hang around here tomorrow. Maybe Audrey, Claudette, and I can find a day trip."

"Good," Matthieu said. "It is settled. You will meet your Jake in Paris; Lu and I will come in a couple of days at the most."

"No, I think Lu is right. I'm fine, Matthieu, don't worry. I will be happy knowing you are going to be on the plane home."

THIRTY-ONE

I pulled my luggage off the train at the *Gare de Lyon* and looked for the taxi station. I'd missed Lu's company on the train trip. Until then, I could distract myself from anticipating Jake by driving to Avignon and dropping off the car. Without Lu to chat with, all I could do for the two-and-a-half-hour train trip was look at the passing scenery, which was not full of *chateaux* or cathedrals, but was long stretches of farmland between train stations. It was disappointing to be on a high-speed train that seemed to travel at the usual speed. The boredom had me imagining the week ahead and anticipating time with Jake without any other interruptions. The fear that I would screw everything up kept me too keyed up to nap.

And now I was standing in a busy French train station, breathless and confused. There were people everywhere and I couldn't figure out where I was going. I should have agreed to Jake picking me up here. I needed a friendly face right now.

I followed the stream of people moving toward the exits, hoping the taxi signs would be obvious, realizing that Lu had taken charge when we arrived, and I'd just followed along. The noise of the city after a week in a small town was like a physical blow. The smell of exhaust mixed with the bitterness of tobacco almost sent me into a coughing fit. I was looking up at a sign for buses, when I heard my name, "Charity? Over here."

I looked and saw Jake standing there dressed like a chauffeur. From the black cap on his head to the white shirt and black pants, he looked delicious. His goofy grin made me smile back at him and I was suddenly running. He dropped the 'Deacon' sign to wrap me in a hug and lift me off my feet. "God, I missed you."

I tried to reply, but my words were cut off by the kiss he planted. I stopped missing Lu and enjoyed the moment.

LATER, when we had said a real hello and I'd unpacked, we sat in delicate metal chairs on the balcony of our suite, looking out over the Mansard roof of the apartments across the street at the Eiffel Tower. I finished telling Jake what Lu and I had accomplished. "How did your meeting go?" I asked, realizing I was monopolizing the conversation.

"Just a second," Jake went into the room and took a bottle out of the mini-bar, champagne. He poured a couple of flutes of bubbly and rejoined me on the balcony. "I got the part."

I toasted him and said, "Tell me all about it, and then I want to go out and celebrate properly with you. Paris awaits us and there are no adults here to tell us what to do. Oh, and remind me to have a *Pastis*. We've been running into it all over the place in the south."

"Okay, before dinner is the best time for *Pastis*. Anyway, I'll still be on location for a couple of months, finishing some extra scenes. Any chance you can stay?"

"I would love to, but I have to get home and find a way to build enough business to support two people." A shadow crossed his face, and I reminded myself to be reasonable. "I promised Lu, and as much as I want to be with you, you'll be working, and I'll be alone most of the time. Do you think that's a good idea? Leaving me to get into trouble? In a place where not everyone believes women should have an opinion?"

The shadow passed as he laughed. "Okay, well that's a point. Maybe Morocco isn't quite ready for you. The good news is that when I get home, I've got at least six months before the next movie starts." He wiggled his eyebrows. Only on him did I think that was cute. "Maybe if Matthieu hasn't moved in with Lu by the time I get back, I can move in with you."

"We'll see. Tell me about the new movie." I pushed aside a bit of panic and reminded myself I was going to trust that Jake wasn't trying to control me.

"Like I said, we should be shooting late in the fall. But you know this business – it could delay for months." He leaned over the edge of the balcony to look down the street. "It's definitely on, though. We'll be filming in Eastern Canada. Maybe a little in New England. Do you think you can arrange to come with me? At least for a few weeks."

"I'll find time. And since it's Canada, Lu and Matthieu can come without jeopardizing his immigration process. If he decides to immigrate, that is."

"Does he have a choice?" Jake turned back to me. "I mean, you've both decided that's what is best. I have no doubt you'll convince him."

"We aren't that controlling," I said, then ducked as he tossed a pillow at me. "Anyway, it means I'll have someone to play with when you are busy. That way we can all stay out of trouble."

Jake drained his glass and pulled me into the room. "You know, you should take some lessons from Lu. She always gets her way without a major battle." He pulled me onto the bed. "Let's go out a bit later. I have something I want to show you."

WANT MORE?

Charity stumbles into a murder scene, and finds a friend in cuffs. Use the QR code to get your copy of Ambition discover who needs Charity's help this time.

Sneak peek on the next page.

If you enjoyed reading Greed, please consider helping other readers to find the story by leaving a review.

CHAPTER 1

I watched as Jake strode across the street and held a gun to the head of a man dressed in black leathers. Just as he reached for the biker's collar, the director shouted, "Cut." Everyone on the set started moving around. Jake rolled his shoulders to relieve the tension of his role before coming back to our side of the street for notes.

He winked at me as he passed. "I told you it might be boring, Charity."

He had no idea how much fun I was having. It might be boring for him. Acting was his job, after all. He would be just as interested if he joined me on a stakeout. At least, that's what I told myself.

Now that Jake and I had found a balance in our relationship – okay, maybe I should say, now that I had learned how to be the happy girlfriend rather than the bitchy one – I could relax and just watch him act. Also, kind of sexy to know that my boyfriend could act the bad-ass but was really a caring guy.

We were filming in New Westminster, the oldest suburb of Metro Vancouver. Down on Front Street, where studios filmed everything from 1940s noir remakes to post-apocalyptic thrillers. Cool and shady, a scent of the working river mixed with the bitterness of diesel from the trains and trucks.

Before I could decide whether to get a snack or go for a walk, wailing sirens caught my attention. A few blocks away three cop cars pulled up in front of what I had assumed was another abandoned storefront. As I watched, the cops entered the building hands on guns. I slipped out of the chair and strolled toward the action.

If there was one thing I found more interesting than watching good looking people act, it was solving crimes, which is why I finally decided to be a private investigator when I grew up. Or, at least, a year ago, I'm not sure I'm grown up yet.

Incoherent shouting drifted down toward me. I heard a woman's voice and then at least two men. I'd heard a few arrests, so I knew that the yelling was an intimidation tactic.

As I listened, wondering what to do, I heard, "Freeze!" Only one word, but what worried me was the escalation in the tone from argument to orders. I had this feeling a witness was needed to keep someone from getting killed.

The woman's voice lost the edge of panic. I could make out the words now that I was closer to the door.

"I didn't do anything."

I knew that voice. It was one I hadn't expected to hear again. One that raised a complicated mix of happiness and annoyance. Val sounded as determined as ever to get her way.

"Put your hands behind your head."

"I called you," she said, anger or frustration sharpening her tone.

"That's fine, now put your hands behind your head." The cop's voice remained calm.

"Look, I didn't kill him. You need to stop hassling me and do your job." Val was mad. The click of handcuffs cut off the next words.

One of the cops escorted Val through the door.

She hadn't changed much in the year since I'd seen her. The hooker clothes had been replaced with a pair of cargo pants and a pale gray tee shirt with a logo too small for me to read. Her hair was bleached and pulled into a tight ponytail, and she looked about ten pounds too thin. The street-smart veneer was still in place as she looked up and met my eyes. A flash of rage before she recognized me. "Charity, what are you doing here?"

She said it as if we'd met in a store. No indication of the situation she was in. She didn't ask for help, but then again, she'd hated having to ask last time. "Hey, Val, what's up?" I tried to match her tone, light and unconcerned, but resentment of how she'd left last time burned.

"Ma'am, please clear the way." The cop shoved Val past me and reached to open the cruiser door.

"What happened?" I wasn't going to let Val disappear again without getting some explanation. "Officer, why is Ms. Wei in cuffs?" I ignored the grin on Val's face. She was in trouble, and acting the smart ass wasn't going to help.

The cop took another step. "Please move away."

I pretended I wasn't intimidated by stiffening my back and standing firm. "I need to know what is happening with Ms. Wei."

"Are you a lawyer?"

"No, but you have her in cuffs, so I assume you aren't just taking her in for questioning."

The cop firmed his lips and gave Val a shove toward the car. He wasn't going to respond.

Val twisted in his grip. "My client was murdered, Charity. They think I did it."

The cop put his hand on Val's head and forced her into the back of the cruiser.

"Is she under arrest?"

He looked at me with narrowed eyes. "No."

He wasn't obligated to tell me anything, let alone the truth. Despite his denial, I could see that Val was going to need representation. "Then she doesn't have to go with you."

"You can tell that to her lawyer."

Val stared at me through the window, the sass and hardness vanished with the slam of the door. The sudden look of fear in her eyes reminding me she was still a teenager. "Val, don't say anything. And don't make the situation any worse. I'll get you a lawyer." I turned back to the cop. "Where are you taking her?"

"The station is on Columbia and 6th. If you get her a lawyer, they'll know what to do." He walked around to the driver's door, got in, and drove away. Val didn't turn to look at me.

I pulled out my phone and then realized that before I found Val some legal help, I needed to know more about what had happened. I looked at the doorway they'd come through. I wasn't hopeful, but, maybe, I could get something before the other cops sent me away.

Stepping quietly across the threshold, I noticed it was some kind of office. Two desks in the open area, a small closed off cubicle and the door to the washroom in the back. No back door. In this part of New West, the back of the building was often bedrock. This didn't look private enough for Val to service a client. I didn't have much hope that she'd found a new way to make money.

One of the remaining cops held up his hand to stop me. "Ma'am, you need to step back outside."

I didn't move, and he wasn't ready to force it. "What happened?"

"Do you know Mr. Schell?"

The other cop put down his radio and moved toward me. "Your name?"

"No, I just... Oh dear." I saw a body in the corner propped into a sitting position. The blood on his chest and the angle of his head confirmed that he wasn't in need of medical attention. I'd seen this kind of thing before, but maybe playing the innocent bystander would get me some sympathy information.

The younger of the two cops walked toward me with his hands spread, like he couldn't decide if he was going to have to catch me as I fainted, or herd me out onto the street. I turned and left before he could get to me.

I put a block between me and the crime scene before I called Lu. "Val's going to be arrested for murder. Can you get her a lawyer?" There was no doubt in my mind that she hadn't done this. The problem was that the cops couldn't risk letting a viable suspect go free. They had to worry about the eventual trial. I only needed to get Val free, which gave me more opportunities.

CHAPTER 2

The next afternoon I sat with Lu in the waiting room of the New West police station. She was my best friend and, despite the fact she didn't really trust Val that much, she'd come to the rescue, sending a lawyer, and paying the bail.

"She's in my custody," Lu reminded me. "She is going have to stay with Matthieu and me until you clear her."

I hoped it would be a matter of hours rather than days. Val could be hard to live with. "Let's just get her side of the story."

Lu looked at me, a frown crossing her face. "How will her side of the story help? Where's her sister? Weren't they both supposed to be leaving the street life? I don't like what she did last time, when she disappeared. How can you trust her?"

Val had come into my life when I agreed to help find her sister. Both of them had been working the streets, both of them teenagers. I thought I was done with defending her a year ago. "How can I just leave her to deal with this alone?"

Lu pursed her lips. "Fine, but don't let her do that again — leave you without a decent goodbye."

I told her that I'd be careful, that I wouldn't expect anything from Val, and that I'd remember how hurt I'd been, no was.

"Okay, but Matthieu should hear this too. I asked him to join us at home so he can meet our new house mate."

Matthieu was a French ex-cop. He'd helped us find a missing woman last year and fallen in love with Lu. Now they were engaged, and he was my business partner.

Before I could respond, Val stepped through a door behind the reception desk. She looked fragile. The clothes she'd been wearing yesterday were wrinkled, and her hair was tangled rather than tied into a neat ponytail. She looked like she hadn't slept for a week. She glanced at me, then Lu, before coming forward.

A policewoman followed closely. "Ms. Cho?" She looked at Lu who nodded. "Ms. Wei is now in your custody. Do you understand what that means?"

"Yes, my lawyer explained it."

"Well, she's all yours. You'll get a call about a court date." The woman turned and disappeared behind the closing door.

"I guess you think I owe you something for bailing me out," Val said. The old attitude was still in place. I found it oddly comforting.

"A thanks would be in order, Val," I said, annoyed that she hadn't learned to accept help with any grace.

She scowled. "Yeah, well, I didn't ask for the bail money. I didn't do anything, so I could have just got a legal aid lawyer and—"

I interrupted what was turning into a tirade of ingratitude. "Val, stop it. We get that you're scared."

"I'm not scared. I'm mad." Val moved past me. "I'm a legit businesswoman now. And you won't be out your money. I'm not skipping on the bail. I'm going to find out who killed my client, and then you'll get the money back. And I'll pay you back for the lawyer."

I took her arm and stopped her from leaving. "Val, you're in Lu's custody. I'll find out who did this."

She pulled away. "No. I need to do it."

Behind the anger, I heard the tears of a frightened young girl.

We took a quick stop at Val's place, an older building in Uptown New Westminster, where she packed a small bag. Val got into Lu's car with a huff that would have been obvious a block away. How she managed to run a business while still maintaining the teenage attitude was beyond me. I retrieved my car from the parking lot and headed over to Lu's home.

WHEN I WALKED through the front door, I heard arguing coming from the kitchen, so I marched in to try to stop it. "What's the problem now?"

Val turned to me. "They narced on you to Jake. He's on his way over."

"Why is he coming over?" I'd hashed it out with him last night. He wasn't happy about it, but he knew Val was important to me, even if he didn't understand why – I didn't really under-stand it myself.

Lu poured a glass of white wine and slid it across the counter toward me. "Matthieu called him. I had nothing to do with it."

"We are making a plan to sort out this mess, yes?" Matthieu asked. "Then Jake is involved. Murder is a dangerous game. It is important that he know what we are doing."

He had more experience than I did, but that didn't mean I liked him jumping in like that. We'd worked together for long enough that Matthieu knew I liked my independence. "So, you thought you'd just step in and make sure the men worked it out?"

He held up his hands in surrender. "You know me better than that, I hope. I simply thought of it and made the call. Now, let us put this aside and think about a plan."

I took a big sip of the wine to calm down. Matthieu really wasn't the type to take over the case. He probably did just think it would be more efficient to make the call as soon as he thought about it. It was done anyway. At least I had some warning.

I saw the worry on Val's face. "Jake likes you, Val. He'll be fine."

"Yeah, I'm not so sure about the liking me bit. At least this time I'm not staying with you. He'll be happy that I'm here in the Cho mansion."

I grinned. "At least here you get a real room. No camping in my living room."

"There are some perks. So, what are we going to do next? I gotta get back to my business soon."

Good question. Our next steps would have to be quick. "Let's wait for Jake. No point in making plans we'd have to explain when he gets here." If the cops thought they had their killer, there would be no investigation. Or there would be one, but it would be into Val's background, and that wouldn't help her get off the charge.

"Look, I don't want to get between you and Jake. I can find the murderer myself. I'm good at investigations." Val stirred the ice in her glass with the straw.

"You can't go without me or someone to watch out for you." Lu started pulling food out of the fridge. "I'm not planning to run around with you when there are two perfectly good investigators right here."

The doorbell interrupted Val's response.

"I'll get it," I said, needing a chance to find out what Jake was going to say before he got involved. I pulled open the door and leaned forward to kiss him. He pecked my cheek and wrapped his arm around me.

"Don't look so worried." He pulled me into a deeper kiss as soon as the door closed behind him. "That's to remind you that I love you in case it gets difficult in there."

"Thanks for giving Val a chance." I wiggled out of his arms and pulled him into the kitchen. "Okay we're all here, let's get planning."

"Not so fast." Jake nodded to Val. "How's it going?"

"Not bad. Well, there's the murder charge, but other than that..."

They all shared a laugh, and then silence. I broke the awkward moment. "We can look into why someone would want this Mr. Schell dead."

"He was a sweet old guy," Val said. "There's no reason for anyone to kill him."

Matthieu pulled out a notebook. "And yet, he is dead."

"It looks like you're ready to start getting down to the job. Why did you call me?" Jake poured a glass of tonic water and pulled one of the stools up to the counter. "I'm no investigator. Neither is Lu."

I looked at Matthieu. "You called him for a reason."

"You are right. I did not take this book out to start investigating. I thought that since this is in the family, so to speak, we should agree on how to start."

"We start by asking questions." Val reached for the notebook. "That's how we found Emma."

"No. We start by agreeing on some ground rules," I said. "That's what Matthieu means. That helps us make the investigation go smoother." At least that was the theory he'd been trying to get me to accept.

"Could you just hire a PI?" Jake asked. "I know you can

both do a good job for strangers. Isn't it like a doctor? They don't work on their family?"

"It doesn't work that way." I hoped.

Matthieu topped up my glass. "In this case, I think Charity is right. Val needs someone who believes in her to lead this investigation. I'm not certain we will be able to find someone who will do that."

Lu placed a plate of snacks on the counter. "Val, you can be a pain, but I don't think you did this. The question is how do we get the cops to believe that?"

Val snorted. "Thanks, I think."

Jake looked at me. "We're all in so let's make this as safe as we can, and as fast as possible. We all have something to get back to. And I think Val is going to get cabin fever staying out here, so you'll need to figure out how to keep her with you."

"She'll travel with me," Matthieu said.

"No, I'm with Charity."

I rolled my eyes. This was going to be a long haul. "We'll stay together, Val. Look, Matthieu, I think it would be better if I took the lead. You can cover our cases."

He concentrated on his notebook for a second. "Yes. Perhaps that is best if this takes more than one or two days. But, I think, that tomorrow I will bring Val with me. I can take her to the lawyer and ensure we all understand what needs to be done."

I could see she was going to argue. "Val, I'll pick you up from there. I can do a bit of research in the morning."

She brushed her glass away. "Fine, but I'm not hiding while you investigate."

If you want to know more, use the QR code to check out AMBITION.

FREE EBOOK

Claim your copy of Buying Into Death when you use the QR code to sign up for my newsletter and follow Charity as she solves her fastest case yet!

ALSO BY P A WILSON

For more books by P A Wilson

Use the QR code below or go to pawilson.ca

ABOUT THE AUTHOR

Perry Wilson is a Canadian author based in Vancouver, BC who has big ideas and an itch to tell stories. Having spent some time on university, a career, and life in general, she returned to writing in 2008 and hasn't looked back since (well, maybe a little, but only while parallel parking).

She is a member of the Vancouver Writers Social Group, The Royal City Literary Arts Society, and The Surrey Writing Workshop. Perry has self-published several novels. She writes the Madeline Journeys, a fantasy series about a high-powered lawyer who finds herself trapped in a magical world, the Quinn Larson Quests, which follows the adventures of a wizard named Quinn who must contend with volatile fae in the heart of Vancouver, and the Charity Deacon Investigations, a mystery thriller series about a private eye who tends to fall into serious trouble with her cases, and The Riverton Romances, a series based in a small town in Oregon, one of her favorite states. Her stand-alone novels are Breaking the Bonds, Closing the Circle, and The Dragon at The Edge of The Map.

For more information
www.pawilson.ca
pawilson@pawilson.ca

ACKNOWLEDGMENTS

People think that the process of writing is solitary. That's not the case for me. I have help from so many people it would be hard to acknowledge everyone, but I'll give it a try.

The support and inspiration I get from my writer's groups is incalculable. The Vancouver Writers Social Group opens my mind to other ways of telling a story. The Royal City Literary Arts Society gives me the opportunity to meet and share with other writers who have more knowledge than I do. The Other 11 Months group is where I learn about getting the words on the page. And my critique group who helps me find the best parts of the story I want to tell. Thanks to all of the members of these great groups.

Last of all, but definitely a huge part of the process, my beta readers. These are the people who love stories and are willing, and more than able, to tell me if my finished story is ready for you, my readers.

www.ingramcontent.com/pod-product-compliance
Lightning Source LLC
Chambersburg PA
CBHW060429180626
46817CB00007B/2738